HOUSE OF CRY

HOUSE OF CRY

A Novel

LINDA BLESER

HARPER LEGEND

HARPER LEGEND

FIRST HARPERCOLLINS PAPERBACK EDITION PUBLISHED IN 2018

Cover design © HarperCollins
Book design by SBI Book Arts, LLC

ISBN 978-0-06-268647-3

For my husband, Jud.
I can't imagine any reality
without you by my side.

HOUSE OF CRY

1

Today is a day of great import.

Jenna liked the sound of that. Maybe one day she'd be a famous poet like her mother. She scribbled the phrase in her journal. Well, it wasn't really a journal, just a drugstore notebook, but it was a special place to share her hopes and fears and secret dreams. The words that had sounded perfect in her head, however, now felt clumsy on paper.

She crossed out the sentence and wrote

Today is a day of destiny.

No, that wasn't right either. How could she put this feeling into words? The day felt ripe with possibility. It had weight, substance, and a sense of wonder. She crossed out the previous sentence and wrote

Today is my thirteenth birthday.

There. That said it all. Today she entered the mysterious world of teenagers. Practically a grown-up.

She stepped into her favorite pair of blue jeans and a T-shirt. Just because she was a teenager didn't mean she couldn't be comfortable. She raked her hair into a ponytail and tiptoed to her bedroom door. She opened it an inch and sniffed, hoping to catch a whiff of bacon and maple syrup. Surely her mother would get up early to make Jenna's favorite breakfast. Wouldn't she?

Jenna sniffed again, but there was no sweetness in the air. Nothing. The house was quiet. Everyone must still be sleeping. Maybe she should just go down and make a bowl of cereal or something. But what if her mother was downstairs wrapping presents or decorating the living room with bright birthday streamers?

She didn't want to spoil the surprise. Instead she went to check on her sister. Cassie's room was all pink and poufy, with a princess bedspread and fluffy marshmallow pillows. It suited her. Cassie was five years younger than Jenna, still a little girl. Her hair fell in perfect golden curls even when she jumped out of bed in the morning. She was just about perfect in every way.

Cassie wasn't in bed. She sat at her little desk, shoulders hunched, arms wrapped protectively over something. "Don't look," she called out as Jenna entered the room.

Jenna covered her eyes, barely hiding the smile on her face. Suddenly she was struck by a sense of déjà vu, the feeling that she'd taken that same step, breathed that same air, and knew exactly what Cassie would say before she opened her mouth.

Then the moment was gone, leaving behind only a sense of wonder.

"One more second . . ." Cassie mumbled.

Jenna peeked through her fingers as Cassie spun around. "There! You can look now." She held out a lumpy object wrapped in a paper napkin and tied with a faded shoelace. "Happy birthday!"

Jenna closed the distance between them and wrapped her arms around Cassie. "Thank you." Then she swiped the clumsily wrapped present from Cassie's hand because—well, because a present was a present after all.

She opened it slowly, surprised when it was completely unwrapped. "Cassie. This is . . ."

"I didn't have any money to buy you a present, and I wanted to give you something special."

"It is special, sweetie." Jenna cradled the plastic figurine in her hand and gazed at the familiar blue jumper and curled pigtails. Dorothy from *The Wizard of Oz*, complete in every detail, right down to the ruby slippers. Cassie had the entire set of figurines from her favorite movie—the Scarecrow, the Tin Man, the Cowardly Lion, and even Glinda the Good Witch. But Dorothy was her favorite. "Are you sure you want to give her up?"

"Well," Cassie shuffled her foot over the carpet, eyes downcast. "I was thinking it might be a birthday *loan*. You can have her for now, then when it's my birthday you can give her back to me. We can trade every year. That way we both get to enjoy her."

"I think that's a wonderful idea," Jenna said, giving her sister another warm hug. Cassie's birthday was a month after Jenna's, so she'd only be giving up her favorite figurine for a few weeks, but it was the thought that counted.

"I'll put it on my bookshelf," Jenna said. "It'll be safe there, and you can come and play with it any time you want, okay?"

Cassie nodded, never taking her eyes from the figurine. It was obvious she missed it already, which made her gift all the more special . . . even if it was more of a loan than an actual gift.

Cassie crinkled her nose and sniffed the air. "Is Mom making you birthday pancakes?"

Jenna shrugged her shoulders. "I don't know. Maybe."

"I'll go check." Cassie scooted out of the room before Jenna could stop her. Not that Jenna would have. She was as anxious to begin the birthday celebration as anyone else. How often did a person became a teenager anyway?

Jenna gazed at the figurine in her hand, rubbing the tip of her thumb over Dorothy's tiny ruby slippers. "There's no place like home," she whispered, then smiled. "Especially on your birthday." Jenna realized that it didn't matter how many birthday gifts she received, this would be her favorite. She tucked Dorothy in her pocket and headed for the door, determined to find out for herself what was taking her sister so long.

As Cassie's bone-chilling scream shattered the air, Jenna realized in an instant that nothing would ever be the same again.

She'd been right the first time:

Today was a day of great import.

2

Twenty years ago today my mother died. To the rest of the world, Marjorie Parker Hall was an award-winning poet. To me she was simply Mom. Her suicide left its thumbprint on the rest of my life, but the damage had been done long before she actually went through with it.

I can see her now, her hair spilling from low-slung ribbons, long tanned legs crossed one over the other with one kitten-heeled sandal dangling like a mesmerist's charm from the tip of her toe. Her cigarette served as punctuation, pointing and circling and jabbing the air as she recited the same line of verse over and over again, words and smoke slipping fluidly from her lips.

I ate corn chips for breakfast while my mother wrote about her life draining away like bloody mother's milk. I lost myself in television fantasies, yearning for chocolate-chip mommies while my own mother butchered tyrants on erasable bond. I think I knew, long before I could put the feeling into words, that I was nothing more than a misplaced modifier in the journal of her life.

An old memory floated to the surface. "Mom? Mom?" I tugged on her sleeve trying to get her attention. "Mom, I can't find my black crayon. Do you know where it is?"

She patted my hand, but there was no comfort in her touch. She stared at a spot over my shoulder. Even when she spoke to me, it was like I wasn't really there. "It's in the grave-yard, honey. That's where all the black crayons go."

No matter how many new boxes I opened, the black cray-ons always disappeared.

Like other neurotic poets before her, my mother was obsessed with death. She danced with it, seduced it like a lover, blanketed it with metaphor, and reeled it in like slip-pery coils of bloody rope. Death was a seedy playground littered with her own words. While my mother constantly courted death, I don't think she ever expected it to be so final.

After she killed herself, I found a handful of black cray-ons scattered in her dresser drawer. I wrapped them up in a rubber band and hid them in my room. For nine months I colored with nothing but black crayons, until they were worn down to paperless nubs too small to grip in my thirteen-year-old hands.

I sat at my desk and ripped the pages from my journal. After tear-ing them into confetti-size pieces, I flushed them down the toi-let. Nothing in my life had permanence, not even the pages of my own journal.

My mother was the writer. She rewrote her life as it unfolded and never finished editing until she was sure her audience would be completely satisfied with the final result. She could produce a waterfall of words that danced and sang and breathed. She carved open her soul and bled onto the paper.

I'm nothing like her. I felt no compulsion to leave a trail of thoughts behind for loved ones and strangers to follow like a trail of bread crumbs. My thoughts were mine and mine alone. Every day was a fresh page with no history to regret and no future to impress.

I'm nothing like my mother.

If I say that often enough, perhaps I'll begin to believe it.

Today is my birthday. As usual, I won't celebrate. It seems vulgar somehow, since today is also the anniversary of my mother's death. I often wonder if she realized the added betrayal of committing suicide on my birthday? Or was she long past the point of caring or even remembering her children existed. Then I feel selfish for thinking she should have considered my feelings in the midst of her pain.

Yet every year the question haunts me. What hurt most was not that she wanted so badly to die but that she couldn't love me enough to live. Then, like my journal entries, I tear up the thought and flush it away.

But I can't erase the image imprinted in my mind—part memory, part nightmare. Was it true or had I embellished it over the years? Could there have been that much blood flowing in a red rush across the black and white kitchen tiles? Did I really see the torn flesh of her wrists pulsing slower and slower as she stretched her arms out, as if begging forgiveness with her final breath? Surely I hadn't watched her die that way. Had I?

And yet I can see the scene as clear as day—Cassie cowering in the corner, her hands covering her eyes in denial, the remnants of her scream still lingering in the air.

I tried to save my mother. I did. I wrapped a dish towel around her wrists, trying to stem the flow of blood, begging her not to leave us. Futile, foolish words tumbled from my lips. "Mommy, don't go. Mommy, please. I'll be good."

The rest is a blur. My father rushed into the room, still in his pajamas. "Jesus, Margie, what have you done?"

He pushed me away. "Take your sister upstairs. Go!"

But I couldn't move, couldn't leave her this way.

He grabbed me under the arms and lifted me away from my mother's side, breaking the spell. "Go now. Get your sister out of here."

That did it. Cassie shouldn't see this. I rushed her upstairs, where we huddled together, and eventually the sirens howled closer and closer. Then silence. We were left alone. Wondering. Waiting.

I rocked Cassie for hours. When I tried to stand, she grabbed my arm, her eyes wide with fear. "Don't go, Jenna. Don't leave me all alonely."

"Never," I promised. "I'll never leave you." *Like she left us.* "Never, Cassie. I promise."

I traced a fingertip along my own wrists. My skin quivered sympathetically. The feeling was one of sensual promise. It would be so easy. So very, very easy. If not for the promise I'd made to Cassie.

The phone rang, but I ignored it. My friends and family knew better than to call with birthday greetings—especially today of all days. Today I turn thirty-three, the exact same age my mother was when she killed herself. If I'm going to do it, today would be the day. The delicious symmetry of following in her bloody footsteps on this day of all days was almost too hard to resist. My fingers clenched, gripping an invisible black crayon the way an ex-smoker reaches for a cigarette before realizing it's no longer there.

When the phone rang again, I decided to get out of the apartment. The rooms felt too small for my dark mood. It happens every year, knocking me off kilter, then lifting again once the day passes. Somehow I always manage to get my balance back. Every year that passes is another victory over whatever self-destructive genes my mother may have passed on to me. But this year was different. This year I felt as if I were at a crossroads.

The sun was ridiculously bright outside after a long winter of gray, sunless skies, promising an early spring thaw. Patches of dirty snow lined the path, stubbornly resisting the killing rays of the sun. Like the stubborn snow, I too resisted the sun's appeal. It was too bright, too real. Sunshine is for the living. It seemed to mock my thoughts, which would be better suited for the invisible night.

I walked with no destination in mind, yet wasn't surprised when I ended up at the cemetery. I often wandered among the gravestones. The solitude suited me. I walked through the gates, beneath the wrought-iron scrollwork—*Mourningkill Cemetery*. It was the one and only place where the name of our town seemed perfectly appropriate.

The stillness was almost peaceful. If not for the rows of markers, I could have been meandering through a park, with its manicured grass and flowering shrubs. Stone benches were scattered throughout the park-like setting, allowing mourners to read, pray, and grieve. I made my way over familiar paths. I had spent enough time in this cemetery to practically recite the names on each individual headstone. Perhaps in a sense I'd been the ghost treading over hallowed ground and haunting the dead all these years.

I passed tombstones of marble and granite and stone, each one like a familiar friend. The monuments were carved with heartfelt inscriptions: loving husband, cherished wife, devoted mother. Till death did they all part.

Saddest of all were the lives cut short too soon. I passed a grave site that always broke my heart—a weeping stone angel prostrate with grief over a tiny carved coffin.

ADDIE ROSE

MAY 14, 2004—SEPTEMBER 1, 2004

FOREVER OUR ANGEL

As always, I said a simple prayer for the child whose time on earth was so brief and the family who would forever mourn their loss. I wondered what little Addie would have become. Doctor, lawyer, tortured poet? All that promise unfulfilled.

I slowly made my way to my mother's graveside. The simple stone marker was unadorned, with a single inscription beneath her name. *Her words live on.*

There was more truth in the engraved words than the more traditional epitaph *Beloved Wife and Mother.*

I wasn't the first to visit her grave today. That came as no surprise. Strangers often visited and left gifts behind—flowers and candles and scribbled tributes. They came seeking wisdom, guidance, and hope. My mother's grave was a mecca for wounded women who felt she understood their pain and spoke for them when they had no voice of their own. Women who thought they knew her. Maybe they do. Maybe they know her better than I ever could.

A slip of paper weighted by a rock caught my eye. I knelt down and reached for it. The page was torn from a book of my mother's poetry. It was creased and worn, as if someone had carried it in a pocket for years. I read the words of my mother's poem and heard her voice beckon from beyond the grave.

HOUSE OF CRY

From six pounds of squalling meat
To six pounds of stone-cold ash
How do you measure a man's life between
Do you count the people he loved
Or those who loved him in return
Is it measured in kisses or tears
By peace or pain or candle prayers
Is it valued for the lives touched along the way
Or nothing more than the measure of time
Lived and died in the House of Cry

I folded the paper and placed it in my pocket. I hoped that whoever had left this poem no longer felt the need to read it and wonder. I hoped that they'd left the darkness behind.

I heard rustling behind me and stood, brushing the grass from my knees. My sister Cassie silently joined me. She glanced once at the headstone, and then turned away. "Here you are."

"How did you find me?"

"Oh," she said with a wave of her hand, "I just followed the dripping trail of misery you left behind."

"Hah. People drip sarcasm. They wallow in misery."

"And you would know, wouldn't you?"

Only Cassie could get away with teasing me on today of all days. I shrugged a shoulder. Maybe I was a little obsessed with death, but who could blame me?

Cassie rolled her eyes. At twenty-seven, she still had the face of a cherub with a halo of golden hair. Even strangers smiled when they passed her on the street.

"Why aren't you at school today?"

Cassie shrugged. "It's spring break. I get a week off from runny noses and screaming rug rats." She said it with a smile. Cassie loved each and every one of her kindergarten students and treated them as if they were her own. She would make a wonderful mother one day.

"So, what was so important that you felt the need to track me down?"

She held out her hand. "I wanted to give you your birthday gift."

I took the faded Dorothy figurine from her with a smile. "Aren't we a little old for this?"

"You're never too old for tradition." Cassie sent a quick, side-long glance to our mother's headstone, then looked away again. "Besides, I have something important to tell you."

I closed my hand around the figurine, squeezing tight as a familiar feeling of déjà vu washed over me.

"I found us a house," she said.

Her statement got my attention. "A house? What for?"

"Well, your apartment is a dump. No offense. And I'm moving out of Dave's place. I thought this would be good for both of us. A fresh start."

I should have been surprised, but I wasn't. Dave was just the latest in a series of broken relationships. Like me, Cassie couldn't—or wouldn't—commit to anything permanent. Maybe she didn't trust people to stay, so she broke things off before they could break her. We all wear our wounds differently. I should know. I was so well protected that even my walls had walls.

"Are we destined to be alone?" I asked.

She smiled. "We're not alone. We always have each other, right?"

"Always. I love you, Cass."

She reached out, then stopped, her hand hovering inches above my wrist. I saw the question in her eyes.

"Don't worry. That's not goodbye."

"I didn't think . . ." She tried to deny it, but the truth was there in her eyes. She'd been searching for signs that I was following too closely in our mother's footsteps. She knew my weakness, and that knowledge was a knife to her heart.

"Yes. You did."

She let out a breath, short and clipped. I wondered how much of my sister's life was spent watching me, searching for signs that I'd leave her, too.

I ran a fingertip along the curved face of our mother's headstone. "Do you ever wonder if we'll end up the same way?"

Cassie looked away. "No, never," she said emphatically.

The tone of her voice stopped me from admitting the truth. I did. All the time, convinced that my mother's mental illness was twisted in the strands of my own DNA. I changed the subject rather than worry her more.

"So, a house, huh? You know a birthday card would have been enough."

"I looked, but I couldn't find one that said, *Happy birthday, sorry your mother's suicide spoiled it for you.*"

With Cassie it was always "your" mother rather than ours. She took my arm and turned us away from the grave without a second glance.

"So, I know how much you enjoy being melancholy on your birthday, but this couldn't wait. There's another person interested in the house, and I promised to bring you by before making an offer. You'll love it." I still hadn't wrapped my head around the idea of the two of us living together. Did that make us old maids now? Were there cats in my future?

"And the best part," she continued, "is that the mortgage would be less than each of us pays for rent. It's a perfect solution."

"I wasn't aware there was a problem needing a solution."

"Well, I need a place to live and you . . ."

"Need a chaperone?"

"No. Nothing like that. I just thought it would be fun, you know?" She nudged my shoulder. "Come on. It'll be a fresh start for both of us."

A fresh start. Why not? It made sense. I'd thought about buying a house before, but it always seemed too permanent somehow. Cassie wasn't the only one with commitment issues.

"So where's this house?"

"About fifteen minutes outside of town. I have my car." Her voice bubbled with excitement. "You'll come look at it?"

I nodded, caught up in her enthusiasm. Hadn't I just said that I felt as if my life were at a crossroads? Maybe this was the new beginning I'd been searching for.

So I went along with Cassie, because she was my first concern. Hadn't it always been that way? Just the two of us against the world.

Our father, distant to begin with, had become nearly invisible after our mother died. He worked long shifts, leaving the two of us to fend for ourselves during the day and most of the evening. Maybe he was dealing with his own grief—or guilt. Maybe he couldn't bear to see his wife's ghost peering out from his daughters' faces. I never asked, and we never spoke her name again.

But my baby sister had always had me. I'd brushed the knots from her hair in the morning, made sloppy peanut butter sandwiches for her lunch, and lulled her to sleep at night with stories of magical kingdoms and fairy queens. I'd walked her to school and wrapped my arms around her when she cried. I could still see the fear in her eyes when she'd begged me not to leave her "all alonely."

Remembering her pet phrase brought a smile to my face. How could I correct her when it seemed so appropriate?

"Never, Cassieboo," I'd promised. "I'll never leave you all alonely."

It was a promise I'd managed to keep . . . so far.

I cast a sideways glance at my sister. She had one hand on the wheel, while the other unconsciously twisted a curl of butter-blond hair around her index finger. It was an endearing habit left over from childhood that always made me smile. I felt unreasonably proud of the woman she'd become. I may not have given birth to Cassie, but I'd practically raised her single-handedly even though I was little more than a child myself.

As if sensing my scrutiny, she glanced over. "You know, I hate your hair dyed black. You're too old for the goth look."

"I'm not going for the goth look." I glanced down at my black pants and black leather jacket. "Well, the tips are better if I blend in with the music crowd at the bar."

Cassie sniffed. "You call that music? It's just a lot of loud noise and head banging if you ask me."

Maybe so, but the truth was it helped me forget. I could get lost in the noise and excitement and energy of the crowd.

"So, about this house . . ."

"I know what you're thinking," Cassie said, her mouth turned down in that defensive pout I recognized so well.

"Do you?"

"Yes, you're thinking this is another harebrained scheme you'll have to talk me out of."

"Not quite. But if the shoe fits . . ."

"You wait and see. You'll love this place."

"And what if I don't?"

"Then I'll just buy it myself," she said, her face set in a stubborn pout. "It's about time I started doing grown-up things like buying a house and tending a garden and . . . stuff."

"Cassie, you realize that gardening will get your hands dirty."

"I'll wear gloves," she shot back, undeterred. "And I'll take a course in home repair and make a budget. I can do it all if I have to."

"I have no doubt you can."

"But I'd rather do it with you." She shot me a mischievous grin. "You don't want me to be all alonely there, do you?"

Her use of the childhood phrase startled me, especially coming right on the heels of that long-ago memory. I don't think either one of us had thought of it in years. Coincidence? It didn't feel like it, any more than it felt like a coincidence that she should drag me to inspect a house only moments after I had read my mother's poem "House of Cry."

They say there's no such thing as coincidence, and a part of me believed that. A strange sense of foreboding washed over me, intensifying as Cassie pulled onto a gravel road. I felt something powerful looming.

Today is a day of great import.

The remembered phrase sent shivers down my spine.

When the house came into view, a rush of recognition washed over me. The unexpected emotion made me even more suspicious, as if I were stepping into a trap.

The house was as charming as Cassie claimed, with a gabled roof, gingerbread trim, and a wraparound porch shaded by an old, old oak. I recognized lilacs that would bloom in a few months and perennial beds circling the grounds. The paint was fresh and the hedges trimmed, all prettied up like a teenage girl on her first date. Sweet and innocent and harmless—which is exactly what Hansel and Gretel must have thought just before the witch tossed them into a hot oven.

Cassie parked behind a car with a real estate logo that matched the for-sale sign posted in the front yard. "This is it," she said.

A breath of air escaped my lips. "Yes. This is it."

The House of Cry.

Cassie shot a questioning glance my way. My cheeks warmed, even though I was sure I hadn't said the words aloud. Maybe she'd heard something in my voice. Or maybe she felt the same strange sense of expectancy as well.

I wanted to tell her to turn around. Something big was going to happen, something that might be terrible or wonderful or both. It didn't make sense, yet the feeling persisted. This *was* the House of Cry, and I'd been sent here for a reason.

Cassie stepped out of the car. "You coming?"

I shook off my apprehension and joined her on the cobbled path leading to the front door. I reached for her hand, and she gave mine a squeeze.

"Ready?" she asked. At my nod, she let go of my hand, then knocked on the door. Whatever we were in for, we'd do it together.

Her knock was answered by a man whose smile immediately put me at ease. "I'm glad you came back," he said to Cassie, then turned to me and held out his hand. "Bob Hartwood, Mourning-kill Real Estate."

"Jenna," I replied. "Jenna Hall."

Something about him seemed familiar. His handshake was warm and brief enough to be professional, but his welcome felt genuine. A lock of dark, wavy hair curled casually against his forehead. He removed his horn-rimmed glasses, and the transformation from Clark Kent to Superman was complete. I found myself feeling ridiculously grateful that I'd splurged on a manicure last week.

"Do we . . . ?" We laughed as we echoed each other's words.

He snapped his fingers. "I know. You tend bar at the Flying Monkey, right?"

"Yes, I do."

"I was there last week," he said. "The band was . . ."

"Magical Muse," I replied. "They're a local indie band."

He nodded, then put his glasses back on, transforming from hot, sexy guy back into hot, nerdy guy. I couldn't decide which was more attractive.

"There's another couple looking at the house," he said. "That's why I told Cassie it was important to get you here as soon as possible."

Was there really another couple interested, or was this just a selling tactic? We stepped inside, and the moment I walked into the house, invisible arms wrapped around me in a warm embrace. It was love at first sight.

Maybe a tiny bit of attraction had rubbed off on the realtor, because when I finally turned to ask him how soon we could move in, I noticed his eyes. They were soft and warm and incredibly appealing. When his gaze caught mine, I was overcome with a sense of recognition. I stumbled, and he reached for my arm. Normally I didn't like being touched and avoided physical contact. *Normally*.

Cassie pulled me away, pointing out one detail after another. I tuned out her voice and let the house's personality speak to me. It

, cozy and warm. A fieldstone fireplace with a solid oak mantle dominated the living room. I immediately envisioned long evenings curled up in front of the fire watching the seasons go by, from the spring lilacs blooming outside the window to Christmas stockings hung from the mantel.

We walked through the rooms, marveling at the personal touches—crown molding, granite counters, and hand-smoothed honey walnut banisters. Each room felt familiar. I knew exactly where the pots would be stored, how many planters to hang between the porch columns, and the angle the morning sun would take as it crept across my bed. Already this house felt like home to me.

More than that, it felt like *my* home.

"Okay, give it to me," Cassie said.

"What?"

"All the reasons why you think this couldn't possibly work. The house is too big, too small, too isolated? Built over a sinkhole? Under power lines? Go ahead, tell me everything that's wrong with the house."

"Nothing," I said. "Absolutely nothing." And it was the truth. I couldn't find a single flaw. The house was warm and welcoming. Every room was exactly as it should be, every window opened to reveal the perfect view. I sensed more than excitement at the prospect of living here. I was hopeful, an emotion almost foreign to me.

For the first time in a long time I had something to focus on, something other than my own misery. "It's perfect," I said, giggling at the look of stunned surprise on Cassie's face. I took my sister's hands and twirled in circles like we had when we were little. "Just perfect!"

3

I asked all the important questions a prospective home buyer was supposed to ask. Like a smitten woman, I wanted to know everything there was to know about my new love, so while Cassie ironed out some details with the agent, I wandered, admiring wood-grained panels and leaded glass windows. Turning a corner in the hallway, I came across a door I hadn't noticed before.

The Doorway to Everwhen.

Huh? Where had that thought come from?

I reached for the doorknob. It was vintage Victorian glass, the old-fashioned kind of doorknob that felt both substantial and elegant. My hand hovered there for a moment while I resisted the impulse to pull away. I felt like I was standing at the crossroads again, torn between the need to step forward and the urge to run away. I grasped the knob and felt a jolt radiating from the center of my chest outward, rippling in waves all the way to my fingertips. The door opened inward to a windowless womb. Empty like the others, yet different somehow.

There was something about the room that drew me. I couldn't remember seeing this room on our walk-through with the real estate agent, and yet I was overcome by an intense familiarity. The first thing that rushed through my mind was *How could I have forgotten it was here?*

It went deeper, as if I'd buried the memory a long, long time ago. There was a sense of rediscovering something I'd lost. My skin tingled and my chest seemed to expand. "Mine," I whispered.

I slid my hand into my pocket and touched the poem I'd found at my mother's grave. It was almost as if she had led me here.

The room was filled with an expectant hush. It seemed to be waiting, ripe with possibilities. I took a hesitant step inside. The air felt thick and fluid at the same time. I reached out to steady myself, fingertips trailing along cool blistered paint as I circled the room, becoming more light headed with each step.

I walked the circumference of the room, feeling a growing sense of ownership with each step, only mildly curious about the incongruity of a round room in the middle of a square house. I spun around in the empty space. My fingertips tingled, and I felt a humming vibration in my ears. Even the air smelled different somehow, as if charged with the electrical currents preceding a thunderstorm. The room seemed to breathe with its own distinctive personality, like a long-forgotten friend.

Inward now, drawn toward the deepest center, I left the safety of the wall and spiraled slowly toward the core. Darkness swirled at the edges of my vision, giving me a curious, unblinking tunnel vision. The darkness pulsed in rhythmic waves. The shadows whispered, but I couldn't make out the words. It didn't matter. Nothing mattered but finding my way to the center and unlocking the room's secrets.

Each step filled me with an increasing sense of serenity, as if I were walking an invisible meditation labyrinth. I couldn't have stopped if I had wanted to; the pull was too strong. I knew, deep down in my soul, that every step I'd taken from my very first breath had led me to this spot in this moment in time.

I found myself moving faster now, rushing to beat the shrinking tunnel of darkness to the center. My thoughts were jumbled, a thousand voices competing for my attention, all of them my own.

Darkness encroached on all sides as I made my way to the heart of the room, where I glimpsed a distant pinpoint of white light. It beckoned and filled me with a desperate yearning. I took one final step into the room's center as darkness obliterated everything, and I tumbled down, down, down into a vast, airless chamber of emptiness.

———————

I don't know how long I was unconscious. When I awoke, dizzy and disoriented, I wasn't afraid. I had only a sense of wonder, as if standing still at the threshold of discovery.

I tried to blink the film from my eyes, but my vision was shrouded by a misty white fog. My eyes felt dry, as if I'd forgotten to blink for the last few hours. *Hours?* Had it been that long? It might have been. It could have been days for all I knew.

The room came into focus one detail at a time, as if being sketched by an artist as I watched. First the walls, complete with dimpled paint and dappled brush strokes, then corners formed with snug baseboards and whitewashed trim. Once the outline was complete, objects appeared. An amber-shaded lamp perched atop a three-legged corner table, an open roll-top desk took shape on the far wall. As I watched, a leather appointment book appeared on the desktop, followed by a porcelain mug from which a dainty plume of steam escaped, almost like an artist's afterthought. Books marched along a sagging shelf, taking shape one after another. I could almost see the titles penned in one letter at a time along the spines.

A woven tapestry took shape on the wall above a moss-green love seat. On another wall hung a framed needlepoint picture with the block-lettered quote *There's No Place Like Home*. An assortment of pillows sprouted like plump blossoms among the grassy cushions. This was unquestionably a woman's study taking shape. But what woman lived here?

I closed my eyes and tried to blink the fantasy away. The room had been empty when I stepped inside. Not just empty, but round. I remembered wondering at the architectural design. Now it was all right angles and sharp corners.

Suddenly I didn't trust my own memory.

I stood up gingerly, half expecting the floor beneath me to dissolve and send me spinning down the rabbit hole. The floor stayed solid beneath my feet, however. Even more surprising than the mysteriously morphing room was the fact that I was wearing a dress. I never wore dresses, preferring the casual comfort of sweatpants or jeans. Even formal occasions simply meant an upscale pantsuit rather than leg-baring skirts or dresses.

Yet here I was in a strange room dressed in a pale-blue wraparound dress like a 1950s sitcom mom. I felt naked and vulnerable. If this was a subconscious fantasy, why would I paint myself in a setting so foreign? Perhaps that was even more disconcerting in a world already gone mad.

Mad. There was the explanation I'd been trying to avoid. Had I finally lost my fragile grip on sanity? It was a destiny I'd been expecting most of my life, like a genetic hand grenade set to explode the moment I released my trembling grip on the pin. Had the time finally arrived? Or had it happened long ago? Maybe none of this was real, and I was sitting somewhere slack jawed and restrained while my tranquilized mind took fantastic journeys into places of my own design.

More questions to push aside for now. How long had I been out? And why hadn't Cassie come looking for me? I'd left her with the real estate agent, hammering out the details for the sale. Surely she was still there—along with my sanity—just a few short steps away. The only thing real was the crumpled poem still clutched in my hand.

I opened the door. Even the hallway seemed different somehow. The walls were blue. Weren't they gray before? Maybe they were grayish blue. I simply couldn't trust my memory. I glanced into rooms fully furnished and wondered if I was having a lucid dream. Certainly I hadn't been unconscious long enough for

Cassie to finalize the deal, paint the walls, then hire a moving va to unload a house full of furniture. Not that I would put it past her.

"Jennie? Is that you, hon?"

I stopped in my tracks. No one called me Jennie. Not anymore.

A sense of foreboding chilled my blood and sent goose bumps skittering over my skin. I turned the corner and faced the last person on earth I ever expected to see.

My mother looked up and smiled. "There you are, Jennie. I thought you were lost."

4

Lost? That's it. I had finally lost it, stepped over the threshold directly into crazy town.

"Mom?" I stared at the apparition before me.

She tipped her head and smiled. "Yes?"

I was transfixed by the sight of her. She had questions in her ears. Not literal questions, but some delicate silvery swirled earrings that looked like question marks. I couldn't take my eyes off them. So instead of asking the big important question—like how my dead mother could be standing right in front of me—I focused on those dangling question marks. Maybe they were symbolic somehow, as if even in my most outlandish fantasy the sight of my mother posed more questions than answers.

"Are you okay, honey? You look as if you'd seen a ghost, for heaven's sake."

A ghost. An apparition. A fantasy. Yeah, something like that.

She put her arm around my shoulder, and the child inside me curled into a fetal position. I wanted to fold into her arms, snuggle on her lap, nuzzle against the pulse at her throat, and drink in the long-forgotten scent of my long-dead mother. Even as the urge struck, I knew it was a false memory. My mother had never held me or rocked me. Where had that treacherous memory come from, then?

Her embrace was casual, as if she'd held me close a thousand times before. As if I wasn't already pulling away, retreating from a closeness that didn't come naturally to me.

I was scared. This couldn't be happening, so the only explanation was that I'd lost my mind. I'd spent my entire life afraid that one day I'd slide into that same black pit my mother fell into and never be able to climb back up the slippery slope to sanity again. I feared that insanity lay hidden in a random gene passed from mother to child, and no matter how hard I tried, I couldn't escape.

Now I had proof.

"I've made you a birthday cake," she said. "We'll wait until your brother comes over before cutting into it, though."

Brother? Okay, the birthday cake I could understand: wishful thinking and all. But a brother?

It took every ounce of strength to force the words from my lips. "I . . . I don't have a brother."

"Now, Jennie, don't start that again. I thought you two patched things up?"

I realized it was pointless to argue. I didn't have a brother, but I didn't have a mother either, and yet here she was standing in front of me. I looked around, desperate for something familiar to latch onto. "Where's Cassie?"

"Hmmm?"

"Cassie? Where is she?" I could feel the hysteria bubbling up in my throat.

My mother gave me a puzzled stare. "Is Cassie a friend you invited over? I'm afraid there's no one here but the two of us."

"Cassie," I murmured. "My sister Cassie."

My mother—or the woman who looked like but couldn't be my mother—shook her head. Her eyes were wary. She leaned forward, and I pulled away. I had no desire to be kissed by a ghost. She gave me the strangest look, then reached up and placed her palm against my forehead.

"Maybe you should go lie down, dear. You still have a bit of a fever."

A fever. That would explain it. I was delirious. Even so, this was the most detailed dream/fantasy/hallucination I'd ever experienced. I decided to roll with it and see what developed. After all, what were my options?

The hand against my brow was cool and comforting. This was the mother I'd always dreamed of and the home I'd always wanted. So what if it was simply a figment of my imagination? Couldn't I just enjoy it while it lasted?

I nodded. "Yes, maybe I should lie down after all."

I turned, eager to escape, but the door I was searching for was no longer there.

"Where's the round room?"

Behind me, I heard my mother's nervous laugh. "There's no round room. Are you sure you haven't been drinking?"

She took my arm and led me in the opposite direction. I wanted to argue. I needed to get back to the door—*the Doorway to Everwhen.*

My mother opened a different door, one far more ordinary than the one I was searching for. "I think it's best if you rest in your own room for now." She entered ahead of me and turned down the covers.

I looked around the room. My room? I remembered seeing this room with Cassie and deciding at that moment it would be my own. But it had been empty then. Now it looked exactly the way I'd imagined it would once I moved into the house. Wasn't that proof that this was simply my own overactive imagination at work? Or was it a memory? No, that was silly. I couldn't have a memory of a room I'd never lived in before.

I sat on the bed, feeling all the fight drain out of me. Sleep. Maybe that was all I needed after all. Maybe if I fell asleep I'd wake up in the real world again.

"I'm fine . . ." I said, unable to force the word "mother" from my lips.

She gave me one long, probing look before bustling out and closing the door behind her. Only then did I get up and begin inspecting the room. I felt like an intruder spying on my own life.

The room was simply furnished, with a bookshelf taking up one entire wall. I didn't recognize any of the covers, and none of the books looked like my preferred reading material. I turned my attention to the desk on the opposite wall. Surely something there would provide clues.

I reached into my pocket and pulled out the ancient figurine Cassie had given me only hours ago. Wasn't that proof enough? I placed the figurine on the desk to remind myself that Cassie existed, despite what the woman claiming to be my mother said.

An iPod was charging on the dresser. I grabbed it, grateful for something familiar to latch onto. I put the headphones on and adjusted the volume. *What the . . . ?*

This certainly wasn't my usual choice of music. It was saccharine sweet. I hit the button, but the next song was just as blah. I sighed and gave in. It was better than nothing. I guessed. After a while I found myself swaying to the music. It was soothing and sweet. Maybe I could get used to it, given enough time. But not today. I yanked the headphones off and tossed the music player back onto the dresser.

Crossing the room, I sat down at the desk, and the first thing that caught my attention was a date book. I opened it, but the only mark on the page was a circle around today's date. I recognized my own handwriting and the words "Happy 33rd Birthday" scribbled in bold red marker. There were no other appointments or clues to be found.

The only other item on the desk was a cell phone. I tugged it from the charger and punched in Cassie's number, but my hopes were dashed when an unfamiliar voice told me to *leave a message and she'd get right back to me.* Not Cassie. Not Cassie's number.

I tossed the cell phone aside and searched the drawers. I pulled out a journal. The pages were covered in my own familiar hand-writing, but the entries chronicled events I had no memory of and mentioned people I didn't know.

I skimmed the pages of a life that was different from but similar to my own. The handwriting was mine but the thoughts and feelings unfamiliar, written by someone other than myself.

A recurring theme was music, but instead of using music to escape and forget, within the pages of this journal it was a bright, unattainable goal. I read passages full of disappointment as rejection and missed opportunities broke the writer's spirit. She wrote about her feelings of failure and waiting for a big break that constantly eluded her. I stopped at a passage that answered one of my questions: who was this brother and what argument had my mother thought we'd "patched up"?

Parker and I had a big fight today. He accused me of being lazy and mooching off mom. He doesn't understand what it's like to have a dream, to want something beside the drudgery of a 9 to 5 job sitting at a desk in a windowless room. Mom understands and encourages me to follow my dream. If I give up now, it will die forever. I hate fighting with Parker, though. I promised him I'd look for a job but that doesn't mean I'm going to give up. I'll never give up. Just like Mom says.

I had to laugh at that. The mother I remembered couldn't even follow through with her own dreams, let alone encourage us to do the same. But at least now I understood the reason for the tension between me and Parker.

I set the journal aside and reached for the yearbook at the bottom of the drawer. I ran my hand over the high-school sym-bol on the faux leather cover. At least this looked familiar. I rifled through the pages, watching a flurry of faces go by, faces I hadn't seen in the last ten years. I felt a jolt of sadness at the friendships I'd let slip away. One face in particular caught my attention—*Diane*. Some friendships had been lost, others destroyed. I closed my eyes, overcome with a sense of guilt, then slammed the book shut and pushed it aside.

In the bottom drawer I found a photo album. Inside were pages filled with scrapbook entries. Again I recognized my own handwriting. The pictures on the pages told the story of a life I didn't remember, pictures of me taken with strangers in unfamiliar places. I saw my mother growing old within the pages, as well as a young boy growing into a man I didn't know. Obviously this was the brother my mother had spoken of, since he was in most of the family photos.

There was a picture of the house standing in the rain. It was titled "Crying House." *No*, I thought. That was wrong. It should be *House of Cry*. Whoever I was, or whoever I'd been, should have known better.

I flipped through the pages, searching desperately for a picture of my sister. It was important that I find some evidence Cassie existed here. Cassie was the force that had kept me tethered to reality all of my life. She was all I'd had when everything else was lost. Cassie was the one thing I'd lived for when I wanted to give up. She had to be here. If not, I knew I was doomed.

There were no answers to be found in this counterfeit life. I'd have to find my own answers. I reached for the journal and turned to a blank page. In block letters I wrote "HOUSE OF CRY" at the top of the page. That's where it had all started, and I instinctively knew I'd find the answers there.

I made a list of everything I could think of, from my dead mother's poem to Cassie telling me about this house. Nothing made sense. I broke it down and did some word association.

What did "house" mean to me? A house is a home, a container for family, for fears, for emotions. A place to feel safe and secure. What about "cry"? We cry when we're lonely, sad, hurt, alone. Babies cry for their mother's comfort and love, for relief from pain or hunger. I could see a connection, but my mind rebelled.

HOUSE OF CRY

Why does the phrase appeal to me? The image is lonely yet proud, as if the act of crying were important enough to deserve a place of its own, like a Native American sweat tent. Need to purge yourself? Spend the night in the House of Cry. Go ahead and get it out of your system. When you're done, put a smile on your face and leave your tears behind. The House of Cry is a place inside ourselves where we can close the door, shutter the windows, and shed the tears we're ashamed to show the world. It's soft and dark inside, and there's a place to lay your head so no one will hear you sobbing.

A knock at the door startled me. I quickly slipped the paper into the desk drawer, then turned with a guilty start to face my mother as she cracked open the door and poked her head into the room. I pasted on a smile and tried valiantly to act normal . . . or whatever version of normal she might be accustomed to.

"Feeling better?" she asked, stepping into the room.

I nodded.

She glanced at the photo album on the desk and smiled, then reached over and flipped through the pages. "This is my favorite picture of the two of us," she said, stopping at a photo with a tropical setting. "We should plan another trip to Cancún one day."

Another trip? I didn't remember the first. Yet there I was, wearing nothing but a golden tan and a string bikini. In the photo my mother's arm rests across my shoulder and mine is wrapped around her waist. We're holding coconut drinks with paper umbrellas. We look happy. Obviously liquor was involved.

I chuckled at my ability to make a joke even under these circumstances. My mother laughed along with me at some shared memory and grasped my shoulder, giving it a familiar caress. My heart beat faster, and together we reminisced over the pages. If she noticed that I wasn't holding up my end of the reminiscing, she didn't mention it.

Looking at the pictures, I realized how much I looked like my mother—the same flashing green eyes, the same crooked smile and wavy caramel hair. Maybe the real reason I'd dyed my hair jet black was not so much to fit in with the punk-rock crowd at the bar as to hide the resemblance to my mother. Seeing the two of us side by side in these photos, smiling and happy, we looked like two peas in a very dysfunctional pod.

I realized this wasn't the mother I remembered, or even the mother I'd wished for. This was a new, improved, and unfamiliar version of the mother who might have been. This was a mother with twice as much life experience as the one my memory held earthbound. But most of all, this was a mother without shadows of death lurking behind her eyes.

And then came the ultimate test. Holding my breath, I forced my gaze to her wrists. They were smooth, unblemished. No scars marked the pale skin. In this world, whatever or wherever it may be, my mother had never slashed her own wrists to escape an unbearable life.

The sigh that escaped my lips held both relief and longing. In a world turned upside down, I began to hope that everything I knew about my past was the dream and this—my mother with unblemished wrists—was the lost reality; that somehow it was my own damaged psyche that had conjured a past where her lifeblood had drained in cooling pools on the black and white kitchen tiles.

When the last page was turned, she patted my shoulder. "Parker's here."

Parker. This was the brother I'd read about in the journal. I wasn't surprised at his name. Parker was my mother's maiden name. She never went by simply Marjorie Hall, but always Marjorie Parker Hall. It made sense she'd pass it on to her firstborn son. Assuming she'd had a son. I knew asking would only raise more suspicions, so I kept silent. Already I was becoming more cunning and secretive. The key to solving this mystery was to remain calm, act normal, and collect as many clues as possible to fill in the missing pieces.

———

Parker was nothing like I expected. I guess I'd assumed he'd be a male version of Cassie—blond and sweet and impish. Instead he was tall, with sandy hair and a hard quality to his unsmiling face. There was no denying we were related, although it was hard to think of him as my brother when we'd just met.

He leaned over and brushed a cool kiss across my cheek. "Happy birthday, Sis."

I smiled and thanked him, hoping I appeared genuine enough. My own reaction surprised me. Instead of shock or outrage, I remained calm. My breath thinned; my pulse slowed. I became watchful. *Let's play along and see what happens.* When confronted by the unbelievable, I found myself searching for clues rather than denying what my own eyes revealed.

Parker handed me a small velvet box wrapped with a scarlet ribbon. "Go ahead and open it," he said.

I glanced at my mother, who nodded, then tugged on the ribbon and opened the jewelry box. Inside was a multifaceted pin in the shape of a tree. There were three gemstones on the main branches. I recognized my own birthstone and my mother's. I could only assume the third stone, ruby red, was Parker's. Three stones representing the only family I seemed to have here.

There was no stone for Cassie. Grief tightened my throat. The fact that she'd never even been born here was a loss worse than death. At least in death a person's memory lived on in the people who loved them. But here, wherever *here* was, no one would know what they'd lost. Everything Cassie had accomplished, the children whose lives she'd changed and everything she'd touched simply ceased to exist. Her existence was erased completely.

Parker cleared his throat, and I realized my silence could be misconstrued as ungratefulness. "It's beautiful," I murmured. I brushed my fingertips over the polished silver. There was something almost magical about the way the delicate branches intertwined, forming an overall pattern, both beautiful and mysterious. The stones formed a perfect triad, each one drawing the eye and then leading it on a circuitous path to the next.

I glanced up at Parker, this time my gratitude sincere. "I really do love it."

"You should," he said, reaching out to unclasp the pin and attach it to my collar. "You've been dropping hints for the last three weeks."

I had? Well, wasn't that a surprise. I'd never been one for coveting jewelry. Nor was I the type of person who felt compelled to drop hints. If I wanted something, I was more likely to run out and get it for myself than wait for someone else to buy it for me. Since I'd never depended on anyone else to take care of my needs, I saw no reason to start now.

I reached up to touch the pin at my collar. Obviously it meant something to the person I pretended to be. And on some deep, subconscious level, it seemed symbolic to me as well.

"Well," my mother said, breaking the spell, "As long as we're opening gifts, you might want to check this out." She handed me a box covered in brightly colored wrapping paper.

I opened the attached card first. The words "Happy birthday to my daughter" caught me by surprise. I should have expected it, but the words still made my stomach tighten and my heart race. Inside, beneath the preprinted greeting, was a handwritten inscription.

> *To my baby girl and best friend on this, your special day. May life always be kind and give you everything you deserve. Love always and forever, Mom.*

Something broke inside me. Emotions I'd held in check for so long rushed to the surface. A shudder raced through my body, and hot tears gathered in my eyes. I quickly bent forward and tore open the package before the tears could fall and give me away.

Inside was a complete set of meditation books and guided imagery CDs. Again I felt a sensation of being split into two separate beings—one a dreamer who enjoyed scrapbooks and meditation, the other a realist who fought off fanciful dreams as signs of an expected mental breakdown. Which one was I really?

I thanked my mother for the gift, not bothering to hide the tears in my eyes. "Awww, honey," she said, wrapping her arms around me. I noticed there were tears in her eyes as well. When had I become such a sappy, sentimental fool? Probably the same day I'd decided to take up meditation.

She sniffed and released me, first patting my hair into place. "In honor of your birthday, I've made your favorite dinner tonight."

Judging by the delightful smells coming from the kitchen, it wasn't Chinese takeout. I wondered what my new favorite dinner might be. When I offered to help, she insisted I sit and relax while she put the final touches on the meal. That left me all alone at the dining room table with Parker.

I remembered the tragic birthday twenty years ago when my expectations for a special birthday breakfast were shattered. That memory felt unreal, however, as if the past I remembered were the dream and this the reality.

Parker poured us each a glass of wine, then interrupted my thoughts with a sarcastic quip. "If I'd known a handful of books and CDs would reduce you to tears, I could have saved a fortune on that silly piece of jewelry you wanted so much."

My hand shot to my collar. I realized I'd unintentionally hurt his feelings. "I'm sorry. I really do love the pin, Parker. Thank you."

"Relax," he said, "I was only teasing. Jeez, you've gotten so serious lately."

Another clue. That meant I wasn't as serious before. I'd have to remember and try to act more . . . well, more like Cassie, I guess. Hadn't I always scolded her for not taking life seriously enough? I worried that Cassie was a little too flighty and fun loving. Maybe that's exactly how I'd have been if I'd grown up without the shadow of my mother's death darkening my every move.

"Are you sure you're all right?" Parker asked.

I touched the rim of my wine glass to his. "Absolutely," I replied. "Just feeling a little sentimental, that's all."

He nodded, but there was a hint of wariness in his eyes. I could tell he didn't quite believe my protests. Maybe there was a reason for his concern. Perhaps in this reality I'd slipped and fallen already and was slowly regaining my mental equilibrium. That would explain why, at the age of thirty-three, I was living here with my mother. Maybe I needed to be watched over.

With a shock, I realized that while I'd checked my mother's wrists, I hadn't checked my own. Had I finally done it? Maybe I was in some kind of afterlife right now. With a surreptitious move, I slid the sleeve of my dress up over my wrists, relieved to find there were no visible signs that they'd been slashed—either in this life or the last. That didn't rule out purgatory, but it was one less thing to worry about.

I rubbed my temples. My head was pounding from all the possibilities running through my mind. There were so many things

I needed to know but didn't dare ask. And the most important question of all: where was Cassie?

I swallowed any questions I might have. The sound of my own voice could break the spell. Instead I remained quiet. Watchful.

Much to my surprise, dinner turned out to be roast duck. How this came to be my favorite is anyone's guess, since, to the best of my knowledge, I'd never tasted duck before. It was obvious my mother had spent hours preparing the dinner, which included mashed potatoes and gravy, tender asparagus, and homemade cornbread. Apparently my mother had taken some cooking classes since I'd seen her last.

The duck was tender on the inside, crispy on the outside, and sinfully greasy. I came back for seconds. If it hadn't been my favorite dinner before, it certainly was now, so it seemed my doppelganger and I had some things in common after all.

After dinner my mother brought out the cake. Before cutting into it, however, she and Parker made a big production out of lighting the candles and actually singing a slightly off-key rendition of "Happy Birthday."

I shot a glance at Parker, not sure which of us was more embarrassed by the display. He grinned and rolled his eyes, as if to say, *Yeah, I know it's silly, but you know how Mom gets a kick out of it.*

I stared at the flickering candles and tried to remember the last time I'd had a birthday cake. I'd banned all celebration of my birthday years ago, including cakes and gifts and sentimental cards.

"Cheer up, Sis. Thirty-three's not so bad. Take it from your older brother."

I swallowed hard. Older brother? How could that be? I was the oldest, then Cassie. I'd just assumed he was younger, too. I couldn't assume anything here. This only proved how easy it would be to make a mistake.

I took a deep breath and blew out the candles, trying to wish myself back to my own familiar world.

———————

After cleaning up the dinner dishes, we took our coffee to the living room. There were pictures on the walls and the mantel over the fireplace. I searched in vain for any sign of Cassie.

With a growing sense of panic, I turned to Parker. "I have to run out for a bit. Can I borrow your car?"

"Sure," he said. "But yours is right out in the driveway. Is something wrong with it?"

"No, I um . . ." *Think fast.* "I'm a little low on gas. Actually now that I think of it, I should be fine. I'll just, uh, grab my keys . . ." I looked around. Where would my keys be?

I caught a look passing between my mother and brother. I knew that look. They were watching me for signs of a mental breakdown. Could it be that even in this seemingly perfect version of my life I was still a lost soul? But that would mean I couldn't blame all of my dark thoughts on the one event that shaped my life. If my mother was still alive, then whom could I blame for everything that's gone wrong?

"Where did I leave my purse?"

My mother pointed to the hallway closet. I turned and rushed to the closet, not caring anymore what they thought. I reached for the first purse I saw hanging inside. If it wasn't mine, I was sure someone would point it out, along with asking more probing questions about whether or not I was feeling all right. I searched inside, and when I found a key ring with a metallic "J" hanging from it, I knew I'd chosen the right one.

"I'll be back soon," I called over my shoulder, although I wasn't completely sure I'd be back at all.

There were three cars in the driveway—a sedate four-door sedan, a fire-engine red convertible, and a little silver Mini Cooper. I headed straight for the Mini and inserted the key, immediately rewarded when the engine turned over. I congratulated myself. I was getting pretty good at this guessing game.

It was only a twenty-minute drive to Cassie's apartment, but it felt like the longest twenty minutes of my life. The streets looked familiar, although now and then I was sure something was different. I almost missed the turn onto Cassie's street because the corner grocery store was now a pet-grooming parlor. Once I got my bearings, however, I found the apartment. Or what used to be Cassie's apartment.

The building was gone, along with the ones on either side of it. They'd paved paradise and put up a parking lot. Well, actually a parking garage, but Joni Mitchell had a better way with lyrics than I did.

This physical evidence was almost more than I could bear. I missed Cassie so much. She was the light to my shadows, the comedy to my tragedy. Without her I felt diminished and incomplete.

Now what? I could have kicked myself for not going back to my room and grabbing the cell phone before I left. There must be someone I could call who would help me straighten out this mess I'd found myself in.

I drove to my apartment, or at least the apartment I remembered living in before my world had turned upside down. I'd no sooner stepped out of the car and started up the sidewalk when the front door opened. Two kids ran out, whooping and hollering, followed by a harried-looking woman who was probably their mother.

"Can I help you?" she asked.

No. No one could help me. Up was down and down was up and I'd fallen into the rabbit hole. "I used to live here."

Her bright smile tightened with suspicion. She glanced at the kids piling into a minivan, then back at me. "I'm on my way out right now. If you'd like to come back some other time . . ."

I scanned the room behind the woman, barely recognizing it as my old apartment. There were toys scattered across the floor, and the walls were painted bright, cheerful colors. It was homey rather than sterile, the way I remembered. "No. That's all right. Thanks anyway." There were no answers for me here.

There was only one place left I could think of to go—the very last place I'd been before my world turned upside down.

I climbed back in the car and drove to Mourningkill Cemetery. This was where I'd found my mother's poem about the House of Cry. This was where I'd begun to lose my way, and every instinct told me this was where I'd find my way back to my real life.

———————————

There's something strangely comforting about walking through a cemetery in daylight. At night, shadows dance over crooked head-stones, lending an air of mystery and magic, and opening a door-way to hauntings and night terrors. During the day, it's harder to believe in ghosts—unless you wake up and find yourself living among them.

I turned a corner and stopped, looking around. Wasn't this the spot where the weeping angel had been? I mentally retraced my steps. Yes, it was right here. Or it had been. Now the stone angel was gone, along with the chiseled tribute to Addie Rose. I would never know what circumstances had taken the child's life or what had changed in this reality to keep her from being buried beneath a weeping angel's wings, but there was a sense of order that I couldn't quite grasp.

The stillness was broken by a lone breeze that captured my attention like a tap on the shoulder. With it came an overwhelming sense of déjà vu. It fled as soon as I concentrated on the feeling, leaving behind a cautionary echo: *remember this moment.*

I moved on and finally reached the spot where I'd stood only a few hours ago, already knowing what I'd find. My mother's grave—or what used to be my mother's grave—had also vanished. Now it was simply an empty plot, waiting to someday become her final resting place. Gone were the candles and flowers and tributes from women who'd been touched by my mother's work. Did I need any further proof that Marjorie Parker Hall was still alive, sitting in her well-lit kitchen waiting for my return?

And yet . . . I reached into my pocket and brushed my fingers over the folded piece of paper. I took a deep breath and pulled it out of my pocket, carefully unfolding the yellowed page. It was my mother's poem "House of Cry," the very poem I'd taken from her grave site only hours ago. Somehow, like Dorothy, the poem had made the journey with me. I clutched it tightly in my fist, desperately holding on to the physical proof of where I'd been.

I felt light-headed and turned to sit on a nearby bench. To my surprise, it was already occupied. I'd been so intent on finding answers on my mother's headstone that I hadn't noticed the woman sitting there when I'd made my way to this spot.

She looked up and smiled. "Hello, Jenna. I was wondering when you'd get here."

5

As the woman on the bench smiled at me, I caught a glimpse of familiar features in an unfamiliar face—a face gently lined and framed with coarse strands of graying hair.

"Do I know you?"

"You did once," she said. "And will again."

Her eyes were clear and ageless, with a clarity that inspired trust and confidence despite her cryptic response. Even her voice, with its deliberate yet musical cadence, came from deep within a half-remembered dream.

I tilted my head as a name tried to fight its way up from a long-buried memory. "Mary . . . ?"

She stood and held out her hand. "Maya," she corrected. "Maya Freemont. I lived down the street from your house when you were just a wee one. Your mother and I were close friends."

Jenna had a vague recollection of a younger version of the woman who stood before her coming to the house and . . .

"You brought a casserole when my mother died."

Maya nodded. "Tuna noodle, if I remember correctly."

"Yes." It could have been ramen noodle for all I remembered, but politeness won out. "Thank you."

"You're welcome."

I caught a whiff of her perfume, a haunting honeysuckle blend that carried with it a memory. Then all the pieces fell into place, and just like that I was thirteen again on the day of my mother's funeral, alone in a sea of adults who were too caught up in their own grief to notice or care that my world had been forever torn into *before* and *after*.

Her warm, strong arms had wrapped me in comfort. "It'll be all right, child. I promise you it'll be all right."

I'd wanted to protest. Even then I knew nothing would ever be all right again. I couldn't speak, however, because her arms held me tighter, and I buried my face against her motherly breast and let loose the tears I'd been trying so hard to keep inside. She'd stroked my hair and let me cry until there was nothing left inside but an immense sense of emptiness.

I haven't cried since that long-ago day.

She reached out, as if to pull me into her arms. The child in me yearned to fall into her embrace once again, but the woman I'd become took an involuntary step back, denying myself the comfort she offered. I knew better now. Words were only a temporary balm.

I took another step back and nearly lost my balance on some loose rocks. I caught myself and looked down at the smooth, unblemished plot of earth where my mother's grave should have been—where it *had* been just this morning before the world turned upside down. I shook my head in confusion. "But my mother's not dead."

"No," Maya said. "She's very much alive, isn't she?"

I took a slow, deep breath. "That doesn't make sense."

"On the contrary," she replied. "When you see the whole picture, everything makes sense." Her gaze came to rest on the pin at my collar. "May I?" she asked, holding out her hand.

I unclasped the pin and handed it to her.

She traced the delicate web of branches in much the same way I had when first seeing it. "Everything you need to know is right here."

I shook my head, uncomprehending.

"Look at these branches," she said, tracing a fingertip over the pin cradled in her palm. "Each one splits off independently, but to understand the tree you must see each individual branch and how it relates to the whole."

I felt a glimmer of something—not quite understanding but a sense that a pattern was beginning to emerge. Before I could grasp it, however, she changed the subject.

"In the center of it all is your House of Cry."

Her use of the phrase from my mother's poem immediately caught my attention. "House of Cry?"

"Well, that's the name you've given it. Everyone calls it something different—a portal, a gateway."

I shivered. "I knew there was something strange about that house."

"It's always strange at first. That's why I'm here. To help you."

"To help me?" I inhaled sharply, struck by the sudden vision of a weeping stone angel. "Who . . . what are you?" A tilt of her head and imperceptible lift of one shoulder dismissed my question. "Whatever you want me to be. Your guardian angel? Your guide? Your higher self? Call me whatever you choose."

I had to smile. The idea of any of those entities revealing themselves as a little black woman with snow in her hair amused me. I guessed that guardian angels or guides could reveal themselves in whatever form gave one comfort. And Maya did just that.

"Is the word really important?" she asked. "The moment you label something you limit all other possibilities." She patted the bench. "Come sit, child."

When I hesitated, she gave me an indulgent smile. "Go ahead and touch me if you'd like."

Feeling foolish, I placed my hand on her shoulder. It was solid. I could feel warmth radiating from her body. If she was an apparition, she was a very convincing one. I slumped to the bench beside her. All the fight drained out of me. I gave up trying to convince myself that reality was waiting just around the corner and opened myself up to whatever mystery my uninvited guest might reveal.

"So," I said. "If you're not a figment of my imagination, then what?"

She shrugged. "A friend."

"I don't . . ." *Have friends*, I was about to say. It sounded melodramatic, but it was the truth. If you don't let people into your heart, they can't hurt you.

She raised a brow, as if I'd spoken aloud.

I folded my arms across my chest. I certainly didn't have to explain myself to this stranger. Or anyone else for that matter.

The look of disappointment on her face cut through my defenses. I didn't know where I was or why. It seemed counterproductive to fight with the only person who might hold some of the answers.

"I want to get back to my own life, my own things," I said, deflated.

"But you just got here."

"I don't even know where *here* is. I want to go home."

"Why? You weren't happy there."

"I was." Even to my own ears, the declaration rang false. "Wasn't I?"

She waited, letting the silence speak for itself. Sure I had my regrets. And maybe I thought if things had been different my life would have been better somehow. That didn't mean I wasn't happy. Concerned, yes. Worried that I might choose the same path my mother did, maybe. Sometimes. Everyone had their own what-ifs, didn't they?

"So this is your chance," she said. "Your chance to find out who you might have been. To answer your own personal what-if."

I shook my head. I didn't want to explore anything. I just wanted to get back to what was familiar.

"There are rules," I argued, still trying to get my feet back on solid ground.

"Really? Who says?"

"Everyone. The universe. There's order and reason and logic. We aren't simply slipped off into alternate realities by some, some . . . *apparition.*

"Maybe," Maya countered, not seeming the least bit insulted to be called an apparition. "Or maybe it's part of human nature to look for order and reason and logic. And maybe it's human nature not to see the very things that challenge the rules they expect."

That was a lot of maybes. My head throbbed. I pressed my palms to my temples to ease the whirling chaos in my brain. "I'm so lost." The sound of my voice held the plaintive cry of a child.

She reached for my hand and cradled it in her own. "That's why I'm here: to help you find your way." She turned my hand and placed the pin on my open palm, then closed my fingers around it. "Everything you need to know is right here."

I wanted answers, but her mystic mumbo jumbo only raised more questions. "None of this makes sense."

"It's your job to make sense of it," she said. "You can spend all your time denying what you're experiencing, but that would be a waste of time better spent understanding why you're here." She released my hand and stood. "Watch," she said. "Watch, listen, and learn."

She started to walk away, then stopped. "Oh, and Jenna?"

I looked up, hoping for some words of wisdom to guide me.

Her eyes twinkled. "Have a happy birthday," she said, then turned and left me alone with the dead.

———

When I drove back to the house, I was relieved to see that Parker's car was no longer in the driveway. I didn't want to deal with him on top of everything else tonight. I walked into the kitchen. It smelled like lemon and cinnamon, prickling familiar sense memories that shouldn't exist. How could I feel so at home in a house that I didn't remember?

I put a kettle on the stove and waited for the water to come to a boil. My mind swirled with questions. Within moments my mother came into the room. Wordlessly she sat at the kitchen table. Without asking, I prepared two cups of tea and joined her. The homey kitchen atmosphere was more conducive to talking than the more formal dining room.

"Parker had to leave," she said, cutting into the leftover cake.

I wasn't sure what to say, so I simply waited.

"He's worried about you." She hesitated, then added, "He seems to think you blame him for everything that's wrong with your life."

Was that possible? In the absence of my mother's tragic suicide, had I shifted all the blame for my failure and unhappiness onto someone else? If so, what did that say about me?

I raised my shoulder in an annoyed shrug. "There's nothing to worry about. I just have a lot on my mind, that's all." For some reason this concern from an older brother I didn't know grated on my nerves. I wondered if he'd been overbearing all of our lives. My reaction felt justifiable. After all, I'd always been the older sibling, the one who took care of everything. I wasn't comfortable giving the title to someone else. As unreasonable as it was, a part of me deeply resented his existence in a world where Cassie wasn't born. I'd traded a sibling I loved for one I didn't even know. It wasn't fair.

There was something else to consider. I couldn't deny that I was unreasonably jealous. Parker hadn't had to struggle in a motherless world. He wasn't constantly reminded that his birthday was a day of mourning rather than a day of celebration. He had all the things I'd been denied—a fantasy mother and a tragedy-free life. He'd stolen what was rightfully mine.

I pushed my annoyance aside and focused on my mother. She'd aged well. At fifty-three, the only lines on her face were laugh lines. I searched the farthest reaches of my memory for my mother's laugh, but all I could come up with was either a self-deprecating sneer or the cries of hysteria from behind locked doors. This mother with clear eyes and a ready smile was foreign to me.

Watch, listen, and learn.

This seemed as good a time as any to start. I swirled the tea bag in my cup, desperately searching my mind for some common ground to start a conversation. The only thing I could come up with was my mother's poetry.

"Have you written any new poems lately?"

She stopped, a forkful of cake halfway to her lips. "Poems? What in the world made you ask that? I haven't written poetry in years. I'm surprised you even remember."

In a world full of surprises, this was the biggest one of all. Writing defined who my mother was. She poured all of her heart and soul into those poems. Marjorie Parker Hall was a flawed human being and an inadequate mother, but she was first and foremost a brilliant poet. I simply couldn't separate the two.

"How could you stop? Writing was everything to you. The most important thing."

For a moment I saw a wistful sadness sweep across her face. There, then gone, replaced by a steel I'd never seen in the mother of my memory.

"You choose what the most important thing in your life is. I had a family to think about. My children were more important."

That simple declaration hurt most of all. Isn't that what I'd always wished for? I remembered as a child tearing up one of my mother's books. I'd ripped the pages out because she cared more about her poetry than she did about me. I'd wanted her to come home, but I knew that the love of one small soul could never compete with the adoration of her readers.

I'd watched the ragged pieces flutter to the floor, and it had felt good at first. It felt as if I were reclaiming my mother somehow. Then it stopped feeling good, but it was too late to put the pages back together again. I scooped them up in a messy pile, my eyes scouring the room in search of a hiding place. My hands slid across the rough oak planks, frantically brushing the tattered pieces into a rounded pile. I barely noticed the splintering wood piercing my finger. When I did, I tugged at the splinter, watching my blood fall like teardrops onto my mother's poetry, hungrily absorbed by her words. The sight mesmerized me. I couldn't put it into words, but somehow I knew it was a sign.

I'd wanted a mother who put me first, before her own pain and sorrow. And yet, that possibility came with its own guilt, as if in gaining a mother I'd robbed the world of its voice. "Are you sorry?" I asked, almost afraid of her answer.

"Sorry? No, not at all. I'm content with the choices I've made."

That was a lie. I could feel the yearning coming off her in waves. She could deny the dream all she wanted, but I wasn't fooled for a moment. Her smile was a mask. I, of all people, knew how much effort it took to keep that mask in place. I knew how exhausting it was to put it on in the morning and what a relief to slip it off at night.

"Do you remember the last poem you wrote?"

She didn't hesitate, and her answer came as no surprise. "It was called 'House of Cry.' I was in a dark, dark place." Her gaze grew distant, as if she were looking far off into the past. "I had to make a very important decision. One I knew would define my life. If I made the wrong choice, I wouldn't be able to live with myself."

"Did you?" I asked. "Did you make the right choice?"

She smiled, and there was no trace of doubt in her eyes. "Absolutely. I made the only choice I could live with."

Choices. I was tempted to show her the poem I still carried in my pocket. But what good would that do?

I unconsciously reached up to my collar and stroked the jeweled branches of the pin my brother had given me. Another clue. I didn't ask about the choice she'd been forced to make. I could see it was personal, and I already felt like an intruder. Whatever it was, it had made the difference between life and death. She hadn't sacrificed her art; she'd chosen a path that stilled the poet's voice inside screaming for release. She'd chosen a life of contentment.

I took her hand in mine. It was a strong hand, a dependable hand. There were still so many questions swirling inside me, but a peaceful calm fell over my heart. I hadn't lost my mother. She existed somewhere in a universe where she'd chosen a path more, rather than less, traveled.

My tea had grown cold, but I drank it anyway to wash away the sweetness of birthday cake on my tongue.

"Why all the questions?" she asked.

"I don't know. I guess birthdays make me nostalgic."

"You've always been one for dwelling on the past."

I had to stifle a snort. At least there was one constant between this life and the one I'd left behind.

"You have to be careful, though, Jennie. It's easy to lose your way if you're always looking behind you instead of watching where you're going. You can't change yesterday. The only thing you can control is what you do today."

I swallowed a snappy retort. There was wisdom in her words. Perhaps the poet inside hadn't been smothered completely. Maybe my mother would find her voice again, only this time the voice would be one of hope rather than despair.

There was one thing I had to know, but I couldn't ask outright. Trying to keep my voice light, I asked if she'd ever thought about having another child.

"I might have," she said. "I'd always wanted a big family. If your father hadn't left . . ." She took a deep breath and let it out with a slow sigh. "I guess it wasn't meant to be. But I can't complain. You and your brother are everything to me. I couldn't ask for better kids."

I wish I could have told her about Cassie, how sweet and pure her soul was, how she could light up a room and make you laugh even when you thought your heart was breaking. About the way she'd sit on the floor with her kindergarten class and make their eyes shine with wonder. But it would be needlessly cruel to tell her about the child she never had. And what good would it do? My mother couldn't go back and change things. None of us can. The only thing we have any control over is today.

We talked for hours. It was simple and sweet, the kind of conversation shared by mothers and daughters around kitchen tables the world over. Like the fictional character in *Flowers for Algernon*, it was only now that I'd experienced this mother/daughter bond that I could truly understand and appreciate what I'd lost when my mother died.

When I finally went to bed, I slept immediately and dreamlessly.

6

I woke up feeling at home—not just in my room but in my body as well. I sat up and stretched, making a closer inspection of my surroundings. The walls were sunny yellow, a color I would never have chosen myself. But it worked in here, especially with the morning sunlight peeking through sheer white lace curtains.

I found myself facing the new day with a sense of wonder and expectation. I hopped out of bed and searched the closet for something that felt more like *me*. I settled for a worn pair of jeans and an eggplant-colored T-shirt. I ran a comb through my hair, free now of the harsh black dye. The natural caramel color complemented my skin. I barely recognized my own face in the mirror. It was softer. The hollows beneath my cheeks were filled in, giving me a rounder, more youthful appearance. I wouldn't go so far as to say I looked happy, but I did look content. That scared me a little. Contentment was dangerous. It meant I had something to lose.

With one last glance at the stranger in the mirror, I turned and followed the sound of singing to the kitchen, where I found my mother cooking breakfast.

"Pancakes?"

She turned. "Oh, there you are, hon. I know you usually grab a yogurt on your way out the door, but I thought you should have something a little more substantial this morning."

How many times as a child had I dreamed of a scene like this? A loving mother making sure I had a warm breakfast before heading off to school. Someone who'd be there waiting for me to come home, to kiss my brow and help me with my homework. Now that

I didn't need mothering anymore, now that I'd learned to survive on my own, she'd finally appeared.

I poured a cup of coffee, then sat down at the table. I raised the cup to my lips at the exact moment my mother nudged the sugar bowl in my direction. I stumbled, realizing my mistake too late to stop. Instead I took a tiny sip of the steaming brew and scowled. "Ugh, I don't think I'll ever get used to drinking it black."

"When did you stop using cream and sugar?"

"Just the other day," I replied. "I thought I'd cut the extra calories out of my diet." It was a small lie compared to the larger lie looming over us—that my dead mother and I were chatting over pancakes and coffee.

The only problem is that the daughter she thinks is sitting across from her has a lifetime of shared memories and experiences. All I have is a vague memory of a mother, a heart full of anger, and questions I can't possibly ask. Questions like *Why did you kill yourself all those years ago?* And the most important question of all, *Could I have done something to save you?*

I'd spent my life screaming at ghosts, but now that my mother was here, I still had no outlet for the anger I'd kept festering inside me all these years. How could I demand explanations for what, in her experience, never happened?

I took a deep breath, consciously pulling myself out of the past and into the present. My mother was dressed in a summer-casual business suit. "Busy day?" I asked.

"Busy week," she replied, setting a steaming plate of pancakes on the table. "It's National Library Week, and we have a full schedule of events. Today I'll be entertaining the fourth-grade class from Mourningkill Elementary School."

So she worked at the library. How appropriate. It made sense that the wordsmith inside her would seek out a place where she was surrounded by books. Did she touch them, run her hands lovingly along the spines while images of unborn poems ran through her mind?

I fondly remembered long hours spent sitting in the library as a young girl, surrounded by volumes of fairy tales where I'd lose myself for hours at a time. I could still remember the thrill of holding my first library card, opening the door to a thousand new worlds, and still felt that same sense of wonder and mystery when I walked through the library doors.

"Sounds like fun," I said. "Mind if I tag along?"

"Of course not, honey. But you have that appointment this morning."

"Appointment?" I stared at my plate, not meeting her eyes. Silver-dollar pancakes swam in a puddle of thick, sweet syrup, the sight of which made my teeth ache.

"Don't tell me you forgot." My mother's voice took on a chiding note. "Parker went to a lot of trouble to get you this job interview. Don't let him down."

Oh, great. Now I had to deal with guilt on top of everything else. Well, at least that explained one of my questions. I was still unemployed, despite my promise to look for a job. And just like I'd read in the journal, Parker was intent on putting me to work and saving me from a life of mooching off my mother.

I'd done a lot of thinking last night about the situation I was in. If I wasn't trapped in a dream, then somehow I'd entered an alternate reality. This life wasn't mine. So whom did it belong to? And where was the displaced soul whose body I now inhabited? When and if I went back to the world I knew, would this reality cease to exist? Or would the person who belonged here come back to find I'd made a mess of her life while she was gone? The possibilities made my brain hurt. I'd have to ask my friend Maya—if I ever saw her again.

She'd told me to watch, listen and learn. That implied a journey, and I clung to the hope that at the end of the journey I'd find myself back where I belonged. Until then, the safest thing to do was to live this life as if it were my own. Trust my own instincts and follow through with any obligations. If that meant going on a job interview, then that's what I'd do. I just had to figure out when and where.

I made a production of looking around the room. "I don't remember where I left the directions."

"Everything's in your briefcase," my mother said. She got up, walked to the closet, and came back with a leather briefcase. She placed it on the table between us with a knowing smile. "So I guess you have everything you need now, right?"

I nodded, eyeing the briefcase. It didn't look like something I'd have picked out. Probably a gift from my ever-helpful brother. I hoped everything I needed was in there. Maybe more. Every little bit of information helped. What kind of job interview would it be? Was I even qualified? In my own world, I was a bartender at a hard-rock lounge. In this world, if I could believe everything written in the journal, I was an aspiring musician. What in the world could I be qualified to do? My mother rested her hand on my shoulder. "Look, I know this isn't exactly what you're looking for. But it pays well and will tide you over until your big break comes along."

She reached for her plate, but I told her I'd clean up. It was the least I could do, since she'd gone out of her way to make breakfast.

She leaned over and pressed a kiss to my forehead. "In that case, I'll head out. Why don't you stop by the library after your interview and let me know how it went?"

"Sounds perfect," I said. "I'll see you then."

As soon as I heard my mother's car pull out of the driveway, I ripped into the briefcase and found a folder with everything I needed for the interview neatly tucked inside. A business card clipped to my resume had an address that would be easy enough to find. I scanned the résumé, surprised to see how unqualified I was for even the most basic entry-level job. My prior work experience included part-time jobs as a waitress, a cashier, and a cake decorator. Even *I* wouldn't hire me.

Reading further, I realized the job I was applying for was a receptionist/typist. Easy enough. I had fair typing skills. Who didn't these days? And I could smile and answer phones. Maybe I *was* qualified for an entry-level job after all. The appointment wasn't for another hour and a half. I had plenty of time to get ready.

First, I needed to do some more investigating. I searched through the briefcase for anything else I could find. There was a day planner inside. I flipped through the addresses, looking for anything familiar, then stopped when I saw my father's name. I hadn't even thought to ask about him. Did this mean he was alive as well? And what would I find if I called? My mother said he'd left when I was a baby. Had we kept in touch? We must have or I wouldn't have his number in my address book. Just one more question to add to the ever-growing pile.

The interview went well. At least I hadn't made a fool of myself or disappointed my brother—surprising how easily that word slipped into place. Since sibling harmony seemed to be important to my mother, I felt I'd accomplished something.

I left the interview and went directly to the library. It was exactly as I remembered. So was the sense of wonder I felt stepping inside. Ever since I was a little girl, this was where I came to escape. It felt real and familiar like no other place on earth ever could.

I wandered down rows, inhaling the heady scent of old books. Each aisle led to endless worlds of mystery, the shelves heavy with promise. As a child I'd fantasized about being locked inside with the entire library to myself. It was a fantasy that still appealed to the little girl in me, the girl who saw the world as a place of end-less possibilities.

Even then I'd preferred being surrounded by books to the company of people, a passive observer rather than a willing par-ticipant. I'd immersed myself in books, refusing to admit the gut-deep desire to write, to invent my own worlds. Admitting that would bind me that much closer to my mother and a fate I des-perately feared.

Even if I'd given in to the temptation, how could I possibly compete with the iconic specter of my own mother. The bar had been set far too high. So I'd soaked in the words of other writers while stifling my own.

I made my way to the poetry section, where I remembered shelves marked *Local Author* that were lined with slim volumes of my mother's work. There were no books of Marjorie Parker Hall's poetry on the shelves, however. Other authors had filled in the spots where she should have been. As much as I'd resented her writing, I felt a sense of sadness and loss.

I remembered sitting quietly in the corner while my mother gave readings at this very library. People would hang on her every word. They hadn't known how much those words had cost her, each one torn from the very depths of her soul. But she'd touched them all. And now it was all gone. Readers around the world would never know what they'd missed.

From my hidden spot, I watched my mother read to a group of students huddled around. Her voice was clear and melodious, bringing the story alive. There was no hint of the words trapped inside her. If she had any regrets, they didn't show. The children's faces were rapt, and I was filled with warmth and pride. The world had lost a poet, but somehow I'd gained a mother. It was a fair trade, at least as far as I was concerned. But at what cost?

It wasn't until she finished reading and the children had scat-tered that I stepped out from my hiding spot. A genuine smile lit up my mother's face when she saw me. Yes, definitely a fair trade. I gave her an impulsive hug. "You're great with kids." I almost said that must be where Cassie got it from but stopped myself.

"I have plenty of experience," she said.

Again I was struck with the sense of having been cheated out of a life that should have been mine. I cleared my throat, fighting back a wave of regret. I'd had enough regrets in my own life. Now it was time to get more information about the one I'd been thrust into. "Any chance I can buy you lunch?"

My mother seemed truly sorry when she told me she couldn't possibly get away for lunch today. My fists tightened as long-held feelings of abandonment resurfaced.

"Maybe another time," she suggested, as casually as if this were just a normal day. For her, it was.

"Maybe," I said, unsure whether I'd even have another day. How much longer would this fantasy last? I could wake up tomorrow and be right back where I'd started—standing all alone over my mother's grave and searching for answers that had died with her. Every moment counted, and I was desperate to make up for all the years I'd lost while I had the chance.

But it wasn't to be. I could see my mother was preoccupied with all she had yet to do. There was no way I could explain without sounding crazy. Since I was working so hard to convince myself that I wasn't, it was important to keep those suspicions to myself.

As if to mock my thoughts, I glanced up and noticed a familiar figure sitting in a far corner of the library with an open book on her lap. *Maya?*

Leaving my mother to her work, I made my way across the room, determined to get some answers out of her this time. Whether she was an angel, a spirit guide, or simply a figment of my imagination, she was here for a reason.

I pulled up a chair and sat across from her, studying her carefully for signs of . . . *what?* Did I expect to see her slowly dissolve or vanish into thin air? Would she change before my very eyes? Sprout wings and fly?

What she actually did was even more shocking. She tapped the sharpened tip of a pencil against her tongue, then began writing on the pages of the open book. A *library* book.

"Maya!" I was horrified. I'd been brought up to respect books, never bend the pages or crack the spine, and above all, never ever write in the margins.

She glanced up and put a finger to her lips, then went back to marking the book on her lap.

"You can't do that," I said, my voice rising an octave.

"Why not? Isn't learning a cumulative process? We build on what we know and benefit from other's experiences as well as their mistakes. I'm simply sharing my thoughts with the next person who reads this book."

She went back to her notations, leaving me both frustrated and confused. I glanced at the open book. Lines were underlined, passages marked with question marks, and doodles drawn along the margins. I leaned over until our foreheads nearly touched. "How long will I be here?"

Maya shrugged. "It depends. Life is unsure, isn't it?"

"That doesn't answer my question."

Her lips curved in a Mona Lisa smile. "I can't answer your questions, Jenna. I can only help you find the answers for yourself."

"Well, I'm not doing a very good job of finding the answers."

"Sometimes if you're not finding the answers, it's because you're not asking the right questions."

"Here's the question I keep coming back to: *What would my life have been like if my mother hadn't selfishly taken her own life and left us all alone?* And now I know. I'm alone and unemployed with a brother I don't get along with and a mother I don't even know." My voice dropped to a whisper. "She doesn't even write poetry anymore."

Maya nodded. "That poetry came from a place of pain and regret. Does your mother seem depressed now?"

I glanced across the room, seeing my mother the way she was today—happy, optimistic, and fulfilled. Unbidden memories come to me. Memories of a happier time before my mother's suicide, when the melancholy slipped away and I caught a glimpse of the woman trapped inside the darkness, moments when she was trying with every ounce of strength in her body to be a good mother and wife, to stitch herself back together again. We'd go to the zoo, and for a little while we looked like any normal family, slipping a quarter into machines for a handful of feed to be lapped up by llamas. I would sit on my mother's lap while she read stories of fairies and trolls that we'd checked out of the library together. I remembered my mother's laughter, rare as it was. How could those memories have slipped away? Why had I focused only on the bad memories when there were so many good ones as well? I'd spent my life coloring her memory with a black crayon, blotting out the good as well as the bad.

"No," I replied. "She seems happy."

So what finally pushed her over the edge? What was it she couldn't live with? That was the answer I was seeking. If I knew that, then maybe I could move on. The only one who knew the answer to that was my mother. As hard as it would be, I knew I'd have to talk to her about that long-ago past when she made a life-changing choice. But not now. There were too many distractions. Tonight, in the privacy of our home, we'd have a heart-to-heart talk. I'd get to know the real person without resentment coloring my understanding.

It still seemed unfair somehow. My mother's poetry had touched so many people. It was a shame to see such talent go to waste. "It's all about choices, isn't it?"

"That's right. Every day we make a multitude of choices," Maya echoed. "Some big, some small. Each one takes you in a different direction, expanding outward in an infinite number of possibilities."

Choices. Hadn't my mother said the very same thing last night? I watched her across the room. I'd been focusing so intently on the differences in my own life that I hadn't even given a thought to her reality. An idea was forming, but it remained elusive, drifting just out of reach. "What about other people's choices? They affect our lives, too, right?"

I turned back to Maya, but she was gone, vanished into thin air. The book she'd been reading sat on the table in front of me. At least it was real. I turned it around and glanced at the notes in the margins. There was a picture of a tree with its branches extending outward and off the pages of the book. It was eerily similar to the pin I wore, the pin that Maya had said was a clue.

I traced the outline, imagining a world of choices, each one setting the story on a different path. The possibilities seemed endless. And what was the sense? Was there only one right path, or was it necessary to experience all of them for the story to be complete?

I closed the book, glancing only briefly at the title: *Doorway to Everwhen.* A chill coursed through me. I was no closer to finding answers, but I felt like I was beginning to hone in on the right questions. The biggest question of all was why my mother was alive and happy in this lifetime. What choices had she made that split her world in two? What was different?

The answer was clear. *Parker* was different. Somehow I knew that he was the key. What was his place in all of this? Was his birth the catalyst that pushed my mother's mental health over the edge somehow? Or was he the one who ultimately saved her?

I needed to talk to my mother about Parker, but how could I approach the subject without raising suspicion? Then it dawned on me. This might be something my father could answer. If nothing else, I needed to find out why he'd left and put together some of the missing pieces to this puzzle. I considered calling him, then decided that I'd rather talk to him face-to-face.

I stopped by my mother's desk and told her I had some errands to run but I'd see her tonight.

"Will you be home for dinner?"

I wasn't sure how long it would take me to get information from my father, or what further directions those clues might lead me in and didn't want to keep her waiting in case I set out on a wild goose chase. "Tell you what," I said. "Why don't I pick up a pizza and a movie for us tonight?"

Her eyes lit up at my suggestion. "That's a wonderful idea." She made as if to give me a hug, but I'd already stepped out of her reach and the moment passed. I just couldn't fake an intimacy I didn't feel. She was my mother, but for all intents and purposes we were strangers.

I checked out the book *Doorway to Everwhen* at the library desk and rushed out the door, nearly bumping into a familiar figure on the sidewalk. A genuine smile sprang to my lips as I recognized the real-estate agent who had shown me and Cassie around the House of Cry. "Hi," I said, holding out my hand. "It's Bob, right? Bob Hartwood?"

Running into him shouldn't have surprised me, since this was the same small town with the same people living here—if you didn't take into consideration those who should be dead. Still, seeing him gave me a jolt, like running into a neighbor when vacationing in a foreign country.

He tilted his head and shot me a puzzled glance, then took my hand. "I'm sorry. Do we know each other?"

"I, um . . ." I suddenly realized how lame it would sound to remind him that he'd shown me a little house in the woods that had a secret room where I'd gone spinning off into some strange parallel reality. He'd think I was crazy, and it was bad enough that one of us was half convinced of that. I had to come up with something vague enough to explain how I knew him. "We met at a mutual friend's party a few months back."

A frown creased his forehead as he searched for recognition. I could see he had no idea who I was and was simply trying to be polite.

"I'm Jenna Hall," I said, as if to jog his memory, although it was clear to me we had never actually met in this timeline. I noticed he was wearing contacts. I kind of missed the nerdy Clark Kent glasses, but he was definitely easy on the eyes without them.

He gave my hand a gentle squeeze and smiled. "Well, it's lovely to meet you, Jenna . . . again." It sounded sincere, and I had the sudden desire to unload everything to someone. He seemed genuinely nice and was probably a good listener. I was tired of being lost and alone in unknown territory.

"Same here," I said, resisting the urge to continue the conversation. His body language told me that even though he didn't remember who I was, he was more than willing to get to know me better now. I knew I was simply grasping at straws. There wasn't anything he could tell me that would help me find my way home. Deflated, I turned to walk away. On a whim I turned back. "Do you sell real estate or do I have you confused with someone else?"

"No, you're right," he said. "But I'm phasing out of real estate and starting a new venture. Why? Are you looking for a house?"

"I might be."

He reached into his pocket and pulled out a business card. "Give me a call," he said, letting his fingers linger over mine for a moment longer than normal. "I'm sure I can find something perfect for you."

"I will," I said, tucking the card into my purse. Up close, his scent was fresh and familiar, like sheets left to dry on a summer breeze. I wanted to linger, to bury my face against his collar and inhale him into my soul. Imagining his arms around me felt natural, like something he'd done hundreds of times.

I was convinced that running into Bob Hartwood again was more than coincidence. He was the gatekeeper, the one who'd led me through the doorway into this new reality. Of course he didn't know that, but it wouldn't stop me from using him to get information. Besides, he was just as handsome as I remembered. And if anything, the attraction was even stronger this time.

I could feel his eyes on me as I walked away. How many times do we run into people that we feel an immediate connection with? How many unfamiliar faces hold a hint of recognition that our logical minds immediately ignore? I found myself wondering if we were all connected in one way or another, simply waiting for the right set of opportunities to find each other all over again.

I shook my head. There were too many questions and not enough answers. An unnamed yearning blossomed deep inside me. I felt the need to connect with someone, even a stranger, for just a little while. All around me people were paired up in laughing groups of two or three. Why was I always alone?

7

I'd only taken two steps when he called my name. I took one more, smiled, then turned and waited. He took a deep breath, and then blurted, "You wouldn't want to join me for a cup of coffee, would you?"

I hesitated. I wanted to see my father, but the thought of spending more time with Bob intrigued me. It would be nice to talk to someone without having to watch every word or accidentally say the wrong thing. While we weren't exactly strangers, he didn't know enough about my personal life to notice if I mentioned a sister who didn't exist or a dead mother who did.

"You'd be doing me a favor," he coaxed. "I just received some good news and have no one to share it with."

"Well, in that case, I'd love to," I said, unable to resist the hopeful expression on his face.

A smile curved his lips, making him look younger and more approachable than when we'd first bumped into each other. We walked a block and a half to the coffee shop, making small talk along the way. I shouldn't have felt so comfortable with a virtual stranger, but I did, and I could sense that he felt the same way. I remembered that same sense of familiarity the first time I'd met him at the doorway to the House of Cry. It was still here. And more. Maybe this sense of connection is what people feel when they talk about meeting their soul mates.

The coffee shop was small and intimate. At the counter we eyed an assortment of homemade muffins the size of softballs.

"Want to split one?" he asked.

"You read my mind. How does blueberry sound to you?"

"Perfect."

We sat at a cozy table drinking coffee from sturdy ceramic mugs while taking turns pinching off bite-sized chunks of blueberry muffin. The aromatic steam and accidental brush of fingertips felt deliciously decadent.

I ran my fingertip over my lips to catch errant muffin crumbs, noticing the way his eyes lingered there. "So, tell me about this good news."

He sat back and took a deep breath. "Have you ever seen a house and known instantly it was meant for you?"

You have no idea. I nodded, trying not to think of the house where we'd first met . . . the house that had brought me here in the first place. There seemed to be a greater force at work here.

"That happened to me recently. I saw this gorgeous old Victorian on a caravan." He stopped to explain. "A caravan is when a group of real-estate agents look at a series of houses currently on the market."

"I see."

"So I saw this house, and I just knew I had to have it. It felt like coming home. Like . . . I don't know. Like meeting your soul mate. Or soul house, I guess. But what does a single guy need with a three-story, seven-bedroom Victorian?"

My heart skipped at the word "soul mate." Had he read my thoughts? And was it my imagination, or had he emphasized the word "single"? Maybe I was reading too much into it. I focused on his words, trying not to be distracted by his lips. My fingers twitched to brush the errant curl that had once again fallen over his forehead.

"See, I've always had this dream of running a bed-and-breakfast. And this place is absolutely perfect. It's nestled in a secluded grove with winding trails lined with shade trees that lead to a small, private lake. The setting is picturesque. The house, on the other hand, is a bit run down. It needs a little TLC and a whole lot of elbow grease. She'll be a real beauty when I'm done with her."

"So, I'm guessing you bought it?"

"My offer was accepted an hour ago." His face lit up like a little boy on Christmas morning.

"Congratulations." I raised my cup in a toast. "To following our dreams."

"Yes," he said, tapping his cup against mine with a solid clink. His gaze lingered for a moment, adding an unspoken layer of meaning when he repeated the phrase "To following our dreams."

I was struck by an intense feeling of déjà vu, as if we'd said those exact words in this very place before. I blinked and the feeling passed, but not the certainty that I was exactly where I was meant to be. And with the person I was meant to be with.

———————

Time passed more quickly than seemed possible. We talked about small-town life, books, and movies. We brainstormed ideas for setting up and running a successful bed-and-breakfast. Before I knew it, hours had gone by. I decided to postpone the trip to my father's house. There was no rush, and I'd promised my mother I'd bring home dinner. I could always visit my father tomorrow . . . assuming I was still trapped in this offshoot reality. I glanced at Bob, torn between wanting to stay in a world where he looked at me the way he was looking at me right now, or finding my way back to the world where I belonged.

I reached out and covered his hand with mine. "Good luck with the bed-and-breakfast. It'll be a lot of work but worth every minute. Every day will be a new adventure."

"That's what I'm hoping," he said, turning his hand and grasping mine. "I plan on stealing some of your ideas, by the way."

"They're all yours, with my blessing."

"I can use all the help I can get. I may have bitten off more than I can chew." He chuckled softly. "Too bad you're not looking for a job."

"As a matter of fact, I may be available."

"Seriously?"

Oh, why not? Maybe this was just the opportunity the "other" me was looking for. And if I was stuck here forever, what better place to land?

"Yes, seriously." I slid my hand from his and rifled through my purse for a scrap of paper. I intended to give him my phone number but realized at the last minute that I had no idea what it was. I stalled for time, digging through my purse while I tried to come up with a solution. Then my fingers brushed against my cell phone.

I pulled it out, nearly shouting *Eureka!* I wasn't out of the woods yet, however. I rolled my eyes. "New contact," I said, hoping that explained my inability to remember my own phone number. I scrolled through the addresses, hoping, hoping . . . YES! I stopped on the address marked "Home" and pressed the call button. I repeated the numbers to Bob as they scrolled across the screen.

He saved the number directly into his own phone, then slipped it back into his pocket. "I'll be in touch," he said. He stood and walked me the few blocks back to my car, although I suspected it might be out of his way. My step felt lighter, the colors around us more vivid.

I unlocked the car, and he held the door for me while I climbed in and strapped on my seat belt. He closed the door and leaned in the window. For a moment I thought he was going to kiss me. It felt so natural, and I was disappointed when he didn't.

"I had a great time," he said. "Thanks for helping me celebrate."

"My pleasure," I said, not wanting to leave. I started the car before it became awkward.

He stepped back. "I'll call. We'll do it again sometime."

"I'd like that." I put the car in drive and pulled away from the curb, watching him in the rearview mirror. He stood there waving until I turned the corner. I glanced at myself in the rearview mirror and was surprised at the goofy smile on my face.

Remembering the promise I'd made to my mother, I stopped at the video store. I had no idea what kind of movie she would like to see, but I was in the mood for a light romantic comedy. Besides, the movie wasn't the point. What mattered was opening up a conversational doorway. I needed to get to know this woman I'd lost so long ago, even if it felt like prying. I picked up a pizza and headed home, anxious to make up for the last twenty motherless years.

———

We curled up on the sofa with the pizza and a pitcher of iced tea. The movie had us laughing like schoolgirls. I hadn't had so much fun in ages. I felt like I was spending the evening with my best friend.

During a particularly tender scene, my mother pointed out the song playing in the background. "That's one of my favorite songs," she said. She glanced toward the piano in the corner. "I love the way you play it."

"Me? I don't . . ." I stopped myself before saying I didn't play piano. Obviously I did or my mother wouldn't have mentioned it. "I don't play very well," I amended.

She gave me an indulgent smile, as if she'd heard that particular argument a hundred times. "Don't be so hard on yourself. You play beautifully. All those years of piano lessons were money well spent."

I looked down at my hands, trying to spy the hidden talent lying dormant inside. They looked like my hands, but they'd been to places I'd never gone, done things I'd only dreamed of doing.

Funny, I'd always wanted to play piano. Why hadn't I pursued that dream? Maybe it was too close to what I considered my mother's right-brained creativity. It was as if I'd needed to build a bridge strong enough to distance myself from the chaos I blamed for my mother's mental destruction.

In doing so, I'd starved the side of myself that yearned for a creative outlet, to sing soulful lyrics or paint pastel landscapes. Most of all I'd silenced the voice that cried out for expression, avoiding any resemblance to the writer who'd given me life. Was I punishing her by turning my back on what she loved most? Or was I protecting myself?

I looked around. This life I haunted was the life I could have had, the person I might have become. I still could. It wasn't too late to gaze into the creative well if I found my way back home. I could even take piano lessons. All I had to do was let go of the legacy I'd assumed for myself. Take off the shackles and become the person I was meant to be.

Somehow I knew that to do so I'd have to let go of the resentment I'd harbored against my mother all these years. It was time to make peace with the ghost of mothers past and embrace the woman she could have become, the woman sitting beside me right now.

This cheerful sunshine mother reminded me of Cassie. Odd. I'd always wondered where Cassie had inherited her sunny disposition. We were so different, my sister and I. She was all light, while I'd inherited my mother's darkness. Or at least that's what I'd thought. Now, seeing this other side of my mother, I wondered if I'd simply worn her dark cloak of depression as a way of keeping her memory close. It seemed as if I didn't take after my mother after all. At least not this smiling, bubbly mother. The one I'd chosen as a role model was the total opposite. The mother I knew hadn't had the chance to become the person she was meant to be. What about me? Could I break the chain as well?

When the movie ended, I wasn't ready for the night to end. I'd spent my life yearning for this kind of connection with my mother, and I wasn't ready to let it go. "You know what I'd like to do?"

"What's that, hon?"

"I'd like to look at home movies. When was the last time we did that?"

She shook her head. "Gosh, we haven't watched home movies in ages. Now where did I . . . ?" She got up and began searching the bookshelf until she found what she was looking for. "Aah, here they are."

She slipped in the first CD and rejoined me on the couch. We sat side by side and watched as my life unfolded before me, from swaddled babe to bouncing toddler to gap-toothed adolescent. My mother was there, smiling in the background, helping me ride a bike without training wheels, and slicing birthday cake after birthday cake, as if to make up for a lifetime of birthdays I'd missed.

I watched Parker grow old as well, mugging for the camera, ripping open Christmas presents with childish delight, and making two-fingered horns behind my head at every opportunity. He was a typical brother in this typical family tableau.

The only thing missing was Cassie.

My mother's eyes glistened with unshed tears. "Sometimes I miss having the two of you running through the house like little hooligans and driving me crazy." She shook her head. "It went by so fast. I can't believe you're all grown up."

I reached for her hand and squeezed gently. The words I yearned to say were trapped inside me. Instead, I asked the only question that seemed to matter. "Are you happy, Mom?"

She tilted her head and looked at me quizzically. "Happy? I'm content. Is that the same thing?"

"I don't know," I said honestly. "Maybe it is."

She reached for me, and this time I didn't pull away. We hugged cheek to cheek and heart to heart. I inhaled deeply, breathing in the scent of my mother. I couldn't bear to spoil the evening by grilling her, despite the questions I needed answers to. Maybe tomorrow, after I talked to my father, I'd be able to pull myself together and do what I had to do. For now I was content to enjoy one enchanted evening in a life that could have been.

8

I was surprised to wake up in the same bedroom in which I'd fallen asleep the night before. Yesterday I'd felt as if I'd awakened into a dream world, a fantasy from which I'd return to my real life. Today this dream felt real, and what I thought of as my old life seemed more like a dream. I was afraid if I stayed here too long I wouldn't know the difference. Or perhaps my old life would simply fade from memory, as dreams tend to do.

I turned and buried my head beneath the pillow. I felt as if I'd accomplished whatever I'd come here to do. I'd made peace with my mother's memory. Hadn't I learned my lesson? By all rights I should be back where I belonged—back in my own world with the sister I loved and the life I'd taken for granted.

As if to taunt me, the alarm went off, mocking me with its persistent ring. I sat up and glared at the offending clock, willing myself to wake up from this dream within a dream. I finally gave up and turned off the alarm. This wasn't a wonderful life, and no matter how often the bell rang, no angels would be getting their wings today.

With a sense of resignation, I climbed out of bed. Not sure what to expect from the day ahead, I tried to find something to wear that would be suitable for any occasion. Ignoring the closet full of ridiculously feminine dresses, I rifled through the dresser drawers looking for something more my style. The best I could come up with was a simple white T-shirt and khaki slacks. I tucked in the T-shirt and pulled the outfit together with a cropped sweater. Pleased with my choice, I turned and let out a cry of surprise when I saw Maya sitting in a chair across from my bed.

"What are you doing here?"

She tipped her head and pushed out her lower lip. "You don't sound happy to see me."

"Of course I'm happy to see you. I just didn't want you to scare my mother." I could hear the shower running in the other room and tried to imagine what would happen if she came out of the bathroom and found Maya there.

"She'd likely die of fright."

I was getting accustomed to Maya's unsettling way of answering my unspoken thoughts. I couldn't help myself. The words just slipped out of my mouth without taking the necessary detour through my brain's censor: "She's already dead."

Maya stood, unfolding like a creaky extension ladder. She gave me a sly wink. "Maybe you need to rethink the meaning of death?"

I had no answer to her comment. Death was death. Either you were here or not. Nothing to it. Except that my mother was somewhere in between. Or maybe I was the one trapped in the in-between.

Speaking of death brought back a vivid memory. "Last night I dreamed I was at my mother's funeral," I said, more to myself than to Maya. "It isn't fair that I'd have to live through that all over again. Wasn't once enough?"

Maya just stared at me, her face soft with understanding.

Bits and pieces of the dream came back to me. It felt so real. My mother had sat up in her coffin and looked straight at me. "You know how it ends, Jennie," she'd said. "Did I do okay?"

I'd answered her as honestly as I could. "Sometimes you made the right choices and sometimes you made the wrong choices. But right or wrong, you did the best you could."

That seemed to be exactly what she wanted to hear. She'd climbed out of her coffin and started walking away. Before she reached the door, she'd turned and said, "I guess that's the best we can hope for."

Maya nodded, as if the dream words had come from her own mouth.

"I'm ready to go home now," I said, cringing at the whine in my voice.

"Really? But you just got here."

Maya moved to my desk. *My* desk. What an odd thought. It wasn't my desk. It belonged to whoever owned this life and all its trappings. Not me. My life was somewhere else. I had to be careful not to lose myself here, where I didn't belong.

"You still have things to do," she said, pulling a book off the shelf and thumbing through it. "You have an appointment with Parker tonight. Oh, and you still wanted to talk to your father, right?"

I nodded.

She turned the book around on the desk. It was my high-school yearbook. The page was opened to the picture of a blond pixie with a mile-wide smile.

"Diane," I said with a shock of remembrance. My chest swelled with emotion as I studied the familiar face. Diane had been my best friend growing up. We'd been inseparable until my mother died. After that, I'd had too many responsibilities, and we'd grown apart.

"We're still friends?"

Maya nodded.

I gazed at the picture, racking my brain. It had been so long since I'd seen Diane in my real world. What did I remember about her? Those years were a blur. I didn't have time for friends after my mother died. I'd pushed away the ones who tried to remain in my life. Maybe on some level I was bitter because I'd had to grow up so fast and miss out on so much of my childhood.

But Diane had kept coming back. Stubborn, that one. Even when I didn't return her calls or made excuses to avoid spending time with her, she'd kept coming back. Until . . .

I remembered the incident that finally ended our friendship for good. It was six years ago. June 23rd, to be exact. Diane had begged me to be in her wedding. At first I'd resisted, but she'd finally broken me down. I'd bought the dress, gone to the rehearsal dinner, done everything I was supposed to do. But on the day of the wedding, I'd bailed at the last minute. Cassie wasn't feeling good that morning. I'd justified my absence that way, but the truth was I couldn't bear being witness to Diane's happiness. It only reminded me of all the things I'd been cheated of in my own life.

Missing her wedding was the final straw. I never heard from Diane again. I hadn't realized until just now how much I missed her. Her absence left a huge void in my life. The saddest part was realizing it was my own fault.

"What happened . . . ?" I glanced up, but Maya was gone. For a moment I wondered if she'd really been there to begin with.

My mother poked her head in the doorway. A towel was wrapped turban style around her wet hair. "Did you say something?"

"Just talking out loud," I replied, then added. "I won't be home for dinner tonight."

"Okay, hon," my mother said, and then disappeared down the hallway.

Once I was sure she was gone, I sat down with the yearbook, studying it page by page. I was surprised to find my picture included in several groups—groups I hadn't had time to join. In my memories I'd had to be home to take care of Cassie, to cook dinner, be mother, father, and nursemaid. Yet here I was in the glee club, cheerleading squad, and drama club. My smiling face was frozen in candid pictures at dances and high-school events. I barely recognized this girl who looked like she didn't have a care in the world. And she didn't, did she? She'd had the time and free-dom to make friends, the chance to grow up normally and dis-cover the person she was meant to be.

I was jealous of this fantasy version of myself. She was so light and carefree, while I was burdened with years of misery. Every single past regret was another weight holding me down. Maybe that was the lesson I was here to learn. Maybe now I could go back to my real life and put things right.

Diane had hijacked an entire page at the back of the yearbook. I smiled as I looked at her familiar looping handwriting, decorated with hearts and stars. She wrote about our friendship and promised that we'd be best friends forever. She detailed our plans to go off to the local community college together and be roommates, then take over the world. How different that was from the life I remembered. I hadn't gone to college; I'd had to work to support Cassie and myself. Diane had gone away to a private school, where she'd met the man she eventually married at the wedding I didn't attend.

In my world, I'd worked three jobs to pay the rent and help with Cassie's tuition so she could follow her dream of becoming a teacher. I had no regrets. She was good at what she did, and the kids loved her. But it wasn't too late for me. Now that Cassie was settled, I could follow my own dreams.

I just had to figure out what they were.

I closed the yearbook, sat yoga-style on the floor, closed my eyes, and tried to make sense of my predicament. Up until now I'd been concentrating on the differences between the life I remembered and the one I'd been thrown into. Maybe I was going about it all wrong. Maybe the answers were hidden in the points of commonality. What remained unchanged? Perhaps those were the markers I needed to focus on.

From what I'd seen so far, the library was unchanged. The cemetery, minus my mother's celebrity marker, remained. And the house, which I mentally referred to as the House of Cry, seemed to be at the center of all of it.

Thinking of the house reminded me of another similarity. Bob Hartwood, the realtor who'd first opened the door to the House of Cry and beckoned me inside. Was it simply coincidence that we had run into each other outside the library, or were we destined to meet? Was there something greater at work here? I could almost see patterns forming from single threads to create a larger tapestry.

I found my father's house easily enough. It was a modest single-family in a suburban development. What surprised me was the fact that he wasn't living there alone. My father had a second family. This was the same man who couldn't be trusted raising two little girls after my mother's death, who left the job of an adult to a thirteen-year-old child. In my wildest dreams, I wouldn't have pegged him as a family man. Yet here was proof—a fenced-in yard littered with bats and balls and Tonka trucks. Good grief, did I have more brothers?

I rang the doorbell, hoping to catch an honest reaction on my father's face that would clue me in to our current relationship. Instead a harried woman answered the door. Her face was clean of makeup, and her hair was pulled back in a no-nonsense ponytail.

"Jenna." She wiped her hands on her pants with more force than necessary, leaving pale, floury streaks on either side. "What are you doing here?" The look on her face made it clear she wasn't happy to see me.

"I, um . . . want to talk to my father."

The woman rolled her eyes. "Of course you do." She shook her head from side to side, her lips pursed with disapproval. "Well, he's not here. You'll have to save your ammunition for another day."

Ammunition?

"I'm tired of you coming around here to beat him up," she said. Her shoulders slumped, and she shook her head. "Let it go, Jenna. The past is the past."

"I just want answers."

"No, you want to make him suffer, and you do that very well. You know he wouldn't turn you away, but then he's miserable for weeks, and the kids and I have to deal with it."

"I'm sorry."

"Let it go. Please. Just take your daddy issues somewhere else and leave us alone."

Daddy issues? I almost laughed in her face. I'd gone from having mother issues in my last life to having father issues in this one. And apparently they were serious enough to turn this sweet-faced woman into a fierce bodyguard.

The woman stood in the doorway, arms folded defensively. I wanted to reassure her that I was no danger to her or her family, but I didn't even know her name.

"Go on back to your mother," she said. There was something in her voice I couldn't put my finger on. Bitterness? "She made her choice a long time ago, and now she has to live with it."

There it was again. It all came down to choices. "I'm sorry," I said again, hoping she'd hear the sincerity behind my words.

She glared at me, unmoved by my apology. Perhaps she'd heard those words before and they hadn't changed anything. Whatever. I knew I'd need more time than I had to heal this rift with my father and his new family.

For everyone's sake, I hoped the door wasn't completely closed. If I couldn't engineer a reconciliation on my own, then maybe my misplaced doppelganger could when she returned to her rightful place in this life.

On the way home I tried to make sense of things. It seemed that even in this world, where I'd had every privilege I'd ever dreamed of, I still wasn't the nice person I appeared to be. I had continued the pattern of blaming other people for my problems: my mother, my brother, and now my father. Maybe it was time to stop blaming other people for my failures and take responsibility for my own life.

————————

I drove around longer than necessary. Soul searching wasn't something that came naturally to me. If anything, I went out of my way to avoid introspection. Maybe up until now I had been afraid of what I'd find if I dug too deep into my own psyche. It was as if I didn't know myself at all.

Then it dawned on me that there was someone who knew me well enough to answer these questions. I pulled the car over and dug through my purse for my cell phone. I scrolled through the numbers, not surprised to find the name I was looking for.

Hadn't Maya made a point of steering me in Diane's direction? Maybe she was trying to tell me something.

Before I could talk myself out of it, I hit the button to dial her number. I closed my eyes and listened to the phone ring. *Please be there, please be there.* When she answered, her voice was the same as I remembered. Tears rushed to my eyes. Only then did I realize how much I'd missed her.

"Diane? This is Jenna. Jenna Hall."

"Well, aren't we formal today?" Her voice held a trace of amusement. "What's up, Jen?"

And just like that, all the years slipped away. I clutched the phone with a trembling hand, seeing her face clearly in my mind—laughing eyes and springy blond curls that refused to be tamed. Memories came rushing back to me—our first day of school, waiting for the school bus together and discovering we both loved the Backstreet Boys and the color purple. We were best friends from

that day forward, inseparable on the playground, doing homework together, and spending the weekends together either at her
house or mine.

I remembered long, lazy summer days at her parents' camp,
sitting on the pier at the lake. We were two skinny, sun-freckled
girls, our freshly painted petal-pink toenails skimming over the
water's surface. Sunlight sparkled across the waves like a legion
of dancing fairies as we whispered secrets in each other's ear,
played truth or dare and "what if?" for hours on end until her
mother called us in for dinner, then stayed awake long into the
night, laughing so hard our sides ached. I'd forgotten all about
those magical days growing up with her constant presence by my
side. Or maybe I'd pushed those memories from my mind so it
wouldn't hurt so much to remember what I'd lost.

How could I have cut her out of my life? I'd been so trapped in
bitterness and jealousy that I'd let something precious slip away.
Was it too late to call on that friendship again? Could I make up
for the years we'd lost? I had to hold onto that glimmer of hope.
I didn't know the woman who called herself my mother, and my
brother was a stranger. Diane was the one constant linking me
from this world to the one I'd left behind. I had to try. "God, it's so
good to hear your voice."

"Are you okay, Jenna? You sound strange."

I wasn't sure how to reply. I cleared my throat. "I just . . . I
really need to talk to you."

"Sure. Come on over. I'll put the coffee on."

Could it be that simple? Obviously the rift in our friendship
had never happened in this reality, but I wasn't sure I knew how to
be a friend anymore. Worse yet, I wasn't sure I knew how to accept
the friendship of another. Maybe that was another lesson I had
been sent here to learn.

I cleared my throat. "Diane, I need to ask you a favor."

"What is it, Jen? You're scaring me. You're not sick, are you?"

"No, it's just . . ." I took a deep breath. "I was hoping we could go someplace for a drink, and my car's acting funny. Would you mind picking me up?" How could I explain that I didn't even know where she lived? Asking for directions to her house would sound crazy. But that was nothing compared to the mountain of crazy I was about to drop on her. If my instincts were right and she was the same dependable person I remembered, then she might be the only one I could count on to help me figure out what was happening. And if I planned on opening that particular can of worms, I'd need more than one drink to work up the courage.

"I'll be right over," she said.

I held onto the phone long after the line went dead. I'd finally found something—someone—to anchor me to my remembered past, and I didn't want to let go.

9

I came home to an empty house. Odd how easily the word "home" slipped off my tongue. This house had felt like home from the first moment I'd set eyes on it. Bob had opened the door, and I'd looked over his shoulder and fallen immediately and hopelessly in love with the house. And here I was having lived a life that I didn't remember, but the feelings were the same. And so was Bob. It was almost as if we were destined to be together.

Me, Bob, and the House of Cry.

I hadn't been home for more than ten minutes when Diane pulled up in the driveway. I met her at the door. Her face was both familiar and different, as if a new set of life memories had altered it in subtle ways. Her hair was lighter than I remembered, with artfully placed highlights, and professionally smoothed and straightened. I missed the wild mass of curls.

It wasn't just her hair that had changed, however. She was smoother than I remembered, more put together, as if she were in a class one step above me. Her handbag alone probably cost more than an entire week's salary at the Flying Monkey—including tips. Despite the obvious differences, I wanted to throw my arms around her and hold on tight, but I knew that would only raise suspicions. In her world we hadn't been estranged for six years.

Diane gave me the once-over. "I thought we were going out?"

I glanced down at the casual outfit I'd managed to rescue from the sea of dresses in the closet, a stark contrast to her fashion-conscious outfit. "I planned on changing. Come help me decide what to wear." I smiled, hoping this was something we'd done a thousand times before. I imagined best friends did things like that all the time.

We chatted as I changed into something more suitable, then pulled my hair out of its usual ponytail and ran a hot iron through the kinks. I added a whisper of mascara and a quick sweep of lip gloss. A glance in the mirror revealed a different reflection than I was accustomed to seeing.

Diane's reflection grinned back at mine. "I don't think I've seen your hair in a ponytail since we were twelve years old."

I gave a half shrug, as if it were no big deal. Diane was as sharp as I remembered. We'd only been together ten minutes, and I'd probably already missed half a dozen nonverbal cues that friends develop over the years. It wasn't going to be easy keeping up the subterfuge for long. She was already calling me out on minor inconsistencies. It wouldn't take her long to notice the big ones.

That might not be a bad thing, however. Maybe Diane was just the person I could talk to about this strange situation I found myself in. And if this turned out to be permanent, it would help to have someone on my side.

"I'll drive," she said, turning to leave. "How about Diablo's?"

"Sounds great," I replied, grabbing my purse and following her out the door.

Diablo's was a family-style restaurant that specialized in hot everything—barbecued ribs, spicy nachos, and hot, hotter, and hottest wings. I was hard pressed to find anything on the menu that wasn't smothered in jalapenos or dripping with hot sauce.

I closed the menu and ordered a salad and my first glass of white zinfandel, knowing I'd need more than one to pull off this charade.

Diane ordered a pomegranate martini. I realized too late that I should have just waited and followed her lead. She sat back and crossed her arms over her chest. "So, what's up?" she asked.

"Nothing," I stammered. "What do you mean?"

She tipped her head and gave me a narrow-eyed stare. "You're acting strange tonight. The hair, the makeup, the whatever the hell you were wearing when I showed up." She threw out her arms in a WTF gesture. "You can't stand Diablo's. It's a running gag between us. I suggest Diablo's, you cross your eyes and make gagging noises, and then we go somewhere else to eat. And white zin? Really? You're the first one to make fun of people who drink white zinfandel."

"Wow, I'm a bitch, huh?"

"No, but you're definitely not yourself tonight."

"You have no idea."

"Try me."

Our drinks came. Just in time. I grabbed my wine and downed it in two quick gulps, then pointed to Diane's glass. "Bring me one of those," I told the waitress before she had a chance to escape. "Please," I added, not caring if politeness was out of character or not. I was about to shatter Diane's image of me anyway.

I took a deep breath for courage and let it out with a sigh of resignation. "What do you do when everything you've always believed in gets turned upside down?"

Diane raised an eyebrow. "Oh good, I'm glad you started with a simple question."

I laughed, breaking the tension. "You're right," I said. "I'm not myself tonight. In fact, I'm not the Jenna you know at all." The wine I'd gulped down went straight to my head, giving me the strength I needed. "I don't even know where to start."

"You know what they say: start at the beginning." She twisted her glass, staring at me in a way that gave nothing away.

"The beginning. Remember how we used to play 'what if?'"
Diane nodded.

"Okay, so pretend we're playing that game." My second drink came, and I took a slow sip, trying to find a way to explain without sounding too crazy. "What if you became trapped in an alternate reality? What if you woke up one day in a world that was kind of like but different from the one you remember?"

"I'd think I was dreaming."

"At first, yeah. But then, when you didn't wake up, you'd start to question your own sanity. You might think you'd gone crazy and everyone around you was sane."

"That's still a possibility." She grinned, taking the sting out of her words.

I'd thought the same thing myself. "But how would I know? It's not as if there's any way I can prove it."

Diane considered it for a moment. "The only way I can think of to prove it is to talk to someone who knows you better than you know yourself. Someone who can tell at a glance if you're lying and call you out on it."

"Someone like you?"

She leaned forward and held my gaze. "Yeah, someone exactly like me."

"You might think I'm crazy."

"It wouldn't be the first time," she said with a laugh.

I caved. The temptation to unload my story to someone was just too great. But I had to get the hardest part over first if I was going to do this. "In my world we're not even friends anymore."

She jerked back, her eyes wide with surprise. "Why not?"

"I let you down. It's a little confusing. In your world you and I went to college together, right?" That was a piece of information I'd uncovered going through the journals in my room.

"Sure, just like we'd always planned."

"Well, in my world that didn't happen. I couldn't afford college after my mother died . . ."

"What?" The shock on her face was real. So was the worry I saw in her eyes. In an instant she'd gone from humoring me to fearing I really had lost my mind. "Your mother died?"

I nodded, tears stinging my eyes. The thought of losing my mother hurt even more now that I'd gotten to know her as an adult instead of through the eyes of an abandoned child.

"Maybe I should just start from the beginning like you said."

Diane must have signaled the waitress when I wasn't looking, because another set of drinks arrived.

"In my world," I said, reaching for more liquid courage, "my mother was a famous poet."

I reached in my purse and pulled out the wrinkled poem I'd taken off her grave. When I'd awakened in this world, the paper was in my pocket. I didn't know how or why it made the trip with me, but I knew it must be important somehow. I straightened out the wrinkles and turned it toward Diane so she could read it.

Her mouth moved as she read the lines to herself. When she finished, she sat back and shook her head. "Your mother wrote this?"

I nodded. "It's pretty typical of her poetry. Dark and depressing, like her. She killed herself when I was thirteen years old, but a legion of women kept her memory alive with regular pilgrimages to her grave. I found this there just before I woke up in this reality."

Diane studied the poem. She gave me a questioning glance but remained silent. Maybe she sensed that any interruption would stop the flow completely, and I'd never get up the courage to finish.

"So after my mother died, I spent most of my time taking care of myself and Cassie."

"Cassie?"

"I have a little sister in my world. No brother. I met Parker for the first time two days ago."

"No big loss," she said. "He was kind of a turd growing up."

I was surprised that I was able to laugh. I had no idea whether or not Diane believed any of what I was saying, but at least she added a bit of levity to the situation. And she hadn't called the people with the white jackets. Not yet anyway.

"So that's why we didn't go to community college together. I couldn't afford college. You went to school out of state, and that's where you met your husband."

Diane's eyes widened. "I have a husband? Is he handsome?" She was humoring me again, but at least she was listening. Whether or not she believed me was less important than getting it off my chest.

"Handsome and charming and witty."

"Oooh, I'm a lucky girl."

"Yes, you are. He worships the ground you walk on."

For just a moment the laughter left her eyes. She frowned. "Don't tease me, Jenna. It's not nice."

"It's true," I said. "He's out there. You just haven't met him because circumstances kept you here instead. In my world, the two of you married six years ago. June 23rd to be exact." I closed my eyes and drew in a deep breath, praying she'd believe me. "One simple choice changes everything. But see, I don't think it's too late. I think that destiny plays a hand in our lives, too. Maybe if we miss one opportunity to meet our soul mate, another opportunity comes along later."

That made me think of Bob. Was he my soul mate? Had we just missed finding each other like Diane and her husband? Or was it just wishful thinking on my part?

"I was supposed to be in your wedding," I said. "But Cassie was sick, and I bailed at the last minute, leaving you in the lurch. I probably could have done things differently. Maybe I was jealous. I don't know. I'm sorry. I'm so sorry."

Diane reached across the table and gripped my hand. "I don't think I'm the one you owe an apology to, since it wasn't *my* wedding you missed."

She was right. Ironic that only my best friend in this reality could tell me how much I needed to make it up to my best friend in the one I'd left behind. I would, too, if I only got the chance.

"So, if I accept your hypothetical premise," Diane said, "then the question is . . . *why*? What's the reason you're here instead of there?"

"That's what I'm trying to figure out." I avoided any mention of Maya. So far Diane had been polite in listening to my rambling story, but throwing in a guardian angel could tip the scales. Better to keep that little tidbit to myself.

"I think I'm here to learn something. You know, I always wondered what my life would have been like if my mother hadn't died. Now I'm finding out, but it's not the fairy tale I'd imagined it would be. My life isn't perfect."

"Whose is?" She reached out and gripped my hand, holding it steadily in her own. "Look, I don't know if you're telling the truth or having a temporary break with reality. But the Jenna I know doesn't just roll over and give up. She's a fighter, and if she wants something bad enough, she'll find a way to get it."

"I'm not the Jenna you know," I replied. "That Jenna was fun-loving and carefree. She had a normal childhood and the freedom to follow her dreams. She didn't let you down on the most important day of your life. She's not resentful and bitter and lonely."

"And tipsy."

I had to laugh. "Yeah, that too."

"Should we order another round?"

"Only if you let me pay for the taxi ride home. We can come back for your car tomorrow."

"It's a deal."

I wasn't sure if we were just lucky to get a singing taxi driver or if he got a contact high off the fumes coming from our pores. Either way, we laughed all the way home. I had no idea whether or not Diane believed a word I said, but it felt good to be able to talk to someone, and for that I was grateful. Simply talking out loud made me start to see connections forming. The connections were still fuzzy, but maybe they'd become clearer with time.

We dropped Diane off first. When we arrived at my house, I gave the taxi driver a generous tip and made my way carefully up the path with one hand digging in my purse for the door key. It wasn't necessary, however. Parker threw open the door and glared at me.

"Hi," I said.

"Did you forget about our appointment?"

"Oops." I edged past him, trying hard not to stumble. It was no surprise I had forgotten about my meeting with Parker. Up until a few days ago, he didn't even exist.

"Typical," he said to my back. "If it's not important to Jenna, then Jenna can't be bothered."

"If it's not important to Jenna, then Jenna can't be bothered," I mimicked sarcastically.

"Very funny. You've been drinking, haven't you?"

"Yeah, I had a few drinks with Diane. So shoot me. I had a rough day. I got told off by Dad's new wife." I snorted. "She wants me to leave him alone."

Parker caught my arm when I stumbled. "When will you learn it's hopeless?" he said. "You can't force him to love you."

I blinked back tears. "But he's our father. Doesn't that count for something?"

Parker shook his head. "He's *your* father. Not mine."

"What?" His words were like a shock of cold water rushing over my drunken haze. And yet somehow this new knowledge didn't surprise me.

Choices.

I unclipped from my blouse the pin Parker had given me and studied the branches. I touched a fingertip to the branch that cradled Parker's birthstone and followed it back to the fork in the trunk. It was starting to make some kind of foggy sense, but I couldn't grasp the concept completely. I clutched the pin tightly in my hand, struggling to think clearly. My stomach rolled and the room spun around me.

"Are you all right?"

I brought a hand to my mouth, fighting a wave of nausea. "Bathroom," I murmured. I turned and stumbled on my way to wash up, grasping the doorknob to keep myself from falling.

I closed the door behind me and took a deep breath. But it wasn't the bathroom I found myself in. "No," I whimpered, looking around at the circular room. "Not yet. I'm just starting to understand."

But it was too late. The room began to spin. I knew what was coming, and as much as I wanted to see Cassie and get back to my real life, I hated the thought of losing the mother I'd just started to know and the friend I'd just found again—a friend who might be the only person willing to believe me.

I'd always been so good at leaving, turning my back on lovers and friends as if they didn't matter. It was important to leave first, leave whole, before I could be shattered by loss. Leaving was what I did best.

But not this time. I wasn't ready to leave. I hadn't even had a chance to say good-bye.

Again.

I tried to fight it, even as I felt my consciousness stretch outward, felt invisible arms reaching out to touch infinity. In that
brief moment before the world faded to black, all the secrets of
the universe seemed just within my grasp. All knowing, all seeing,
all understanding. I knew something . . . everything. And then the
knowing was gone, leaving nothing but endless night in its wake.

10

I came awake slowly, as if drifting upward from a dream. Before I'd even opened my eyes, I could sense that everything had changed. The events of the last few days already felt unreal, almost dream-like. I wanted to close my eyes and slip back into the dream to see where it would take me. I'd just reconnected with my best friend, found the mother I was meant to know, and discovered a big brother who cared enough about my feelings to buy me something he knew I wanted even though we butted heads at every opportunity.

Then there was Bob. My chest tightened, mourning the loss of a new romance that hadn't had the chance to blossom. We'd had a lovely conversation, ripe with the promise of many more to come. Couldn't I just enjoy it for a little while before being thrown into a new unknown?

My head spun, as if I'd had too much to drink. But wait. Wasn't that part of the dream as well? I tried to stand, but the room spun around me. I clenched my fists, then cried out as a sharp pain stabbed my palm. I opened my hand, surprised to find the tree-shaped jewelry Parker had given me as a birthday gift. Even in my confused state, I knew it wasn't possible to take items from within a dream, no matter how real it felt. Then what? Before I could answer my own question, the door opened.

"Oh, Jen, are you okay?"

I reached up and rubbed a lump on the back of my head, wincing at the pain. "Yeah, I just . . ." I stopped and stared. "Bob?"

He knelt down and brushed a finger over my temple. "You're bleeding. What happened?"

"I, um . . . I fell." What was Bob doing here? Was I back at the beginning? Was Cassie in the other room waiting for me to make an offer on the house? I glanced at the pin again, trying to piece it all together.

Bob followed my gaze to the pin in my hand. "Where did you get that?"

"Parker gave it to me."

"Parker?"

"My brother." Too late I realized my mistake.

"You don't have a brother," Bob said, brushing his fingertips over the growing lump on my head. His brow creased in worry lines. "You must have really hit your head hard."

I nodded. The pain went deeper than a superficial wound. The mother I was getting to know was gone. I'd just found her, and I'd lost her already. You'd think that having already spent the last twenty years mourning would take some of the edge off, but letting go of the fantasy brought a different kind of pain. Instead of a loss of innocence, this was a loss of possibilities.

I wanted to ask about Cassie, but I was afraid to say anything. Bob reached under my arms and helped me to my feet. I stumbled against him, and he wrapped his arms around me. I rested my head against his shoulder for a moment, trying to regain my equilibrium, and breathed in his scent. If yesterday wasn't real, then why was his scent so intimately familiar? Surely this was even more evidence that our time together wasn't simply a dream but some form of alternate reality. So where was I now?

I looked around for something familiar to latch onto, but it was an ordinary bathroom, with nothing to distinguish it from any other. When I wobbled in Bob's arms, he scooped me up and carried me to the bedroom. I collapsed against his chest, feeling so right, as if he'd carried me like this a thousand times before.

The bedroom felt more personal. Little touches here and there seemed familiar—not as if I'd been here before, but familiar in the sense that if I'd designed the perfect romantic getaway, it would look exactly like this room. The walls were a soft sea blue, and cloud-like curtains billowed on a gentle breeze from the open window. Everything felt inviting, from the plump love seat tucked into a corner to the delicate pillowcases trimmed in eyelet lace that adorned the bed.

And there was Bob, handsome and gallant. If not every woman's dream, he was definitely mine.

Mine.

A feeling of possessiveness washed over me. I wanted Bob. I wanted to share his hopes, his dreams, his life. And now it looked as though I was. Or was it all wishful thinking on my part? A fantasy I'd created in a fevered dream.

Bob set me gently on the bed, where I sank onto a soft down comforter. I felt weightless and pampered, transported from one dream into another. But if this was a dream, I never wanted to wake up.

I turned my head to the side and snuggled into the pillows. That's when I caught sight of the framed photo on the bedside table—a dashing groom in a dark tuxedo and his glowing bride in ivory lace. It was a wedding photo of Bob . . . and me!

My skin grew cold, and I felt the blood rush from my head. I took a deep breath, trying desperately to hold on, but it was useless. For the second time in less than an hour, a black nothingness rushed over me, washing everything else away.

I heard hushed voices. "Mild concussion. We'll keep her overnight for observation . . ." I kept my eyes closed, trying to gather my thoughts. I knew it wasn't a concussion, but shock, that had brought me here. Obviously I'd slipped into another alternate reality.

But how? And why? And what about Parker's pin? Was that proof that both realities were real?

Now that I thought about it, when I'd awakened in the secret room the first time, I still held the poem I'd taken from my mother's grave, along with Cassie's statue of Dorothy. I'd left them both behind. But the pin was still here. Perhaps anything I held or wore stayed with me from one reality to the next.

Either way, the best I could do was to go with it until I could figure things out. But how could I pretend an intimate history with someone I'd just met? There was no way I could fool a man I'd been married to for . . . how long? He'd know things about me that I didn't even know myself. There was no possible way I could pull this off.

Then it came to me. If the doctors said I was probably suffering from a concussion, all I had to do was pretend to have a little temporary amnesia while I interrogated Bob for information about this new world I'd dropped into. It would be easy enough to act confused. Everyone would blame it on a head injury, giving me the freedom to find what I needed.

And I knew right where to start. If this Jenna was anything like the last two, there'd be journals somewhere. Once I found them, I'd have a better understanding of my place here. More importantly, I needed to know everything about Bob—how we met, how long we dated, when we fell in love, where he proposed, our first kiss, and the first time we made love. Oh. Maybe I'd better think about that later.

I heard footsteps coming closer, then felt movement by my bed. I knew Bob was there watching me. He reached over and closed his hand around mine. My eyelids fluttered open, and I nearly gasped at the tenderness in his eyes. I had never imagined a man would ever look at me that way.

"Hey there," he said with a worried smile. "You gave me a scare."

"I'm sorry."

He brushed his fingers over my knuckles. "How do you feel?"

"Groggy." At least I could be honest about that. I reached up and touched his glasses. "Have you ever thought about getting contacts?"

He chuckled. "No, I thought about it, but you said you liked sleeping with both Clark Kent *and* Superman."

I smiled. Yeah, that sounded just like me.

He turned my hand in his and frowned. "Where's your wedding band?"

I shrugged. "I don't know." That, too, was the truth. "Maybe I left it on the sink when I was washing my hands?" I suppose that shouldn't have come out as a question, but Bob didn't seem to notice. "I don't remember a lot of things," I said.

"That's okay. I think that's normal with head injuries. I'm sure it's only temporary."

"What if it's not?" I murmured. "Will you help me remember?"

"Of course I will. I'll tell you anything you want to know."

"I want to know everything," I said. "Everything about us."

"Lucky for you, that's my favorite story." Bob leaned forward, resting his elbows on the side of the bed. "It all started when my best friend fell in love. At first I was a little jealous because my buddy was suddenly too busy to party. All he cared about was this new girl he had met at college. It was Diane this and Diane that . . ."

My eyes widened. Could it be the same Diane?

"I'm not ashamed to admit I was jealous. But then I met Diane, and she was just as wonderful as he'd told me she was, and they were perfect for each other. How could I be jealous when my best friend had found his soul mate?"

"You believe in soul mates?"

He smiled tenderly. "I do now."

My heart skittered, then resumed its normal beat.

"So guess who was best man at their wedding?"

It was all starting to come together. "That would be you, right?"

"That's right. And guess who just happened to be the bride's maid of honor?"

"That would be me?"

He leaned forward and kissed the tip of my nose. "Right again. It was love at first sight. Well, it was for me. You had other things on your mind."

I thought back to that night. In my world, I hadn't gone to Diane's wedding because Cassie was sick and I didn't want to leave her alone. One little change and my life had gone in an entirely different direction. I'd stayed home that day and hadn't met the love of my life. "Cassie was sick."

He looked away. I didn't have the advantage of knowing Bob all those years, but it was obvious to me that he was hiding something. "That's right," he said. "Cassie was sick, and you were worried about having left her. But it wasn't your fault." He frowned and stared at me, as if he'd given me this lecture a thousand times before. "She was old enough to fend for herself for a few hours."

"What wasn't my fault?" I tried to sit up. "What happened to Cassie?" Was she hurt? Dead? What had I done? I knew I shouldn't have left her alone that night. Even if it meant never meeting Bob, never getting married and having the life I'd always dreamed of. Not at my sister's expense.

"What happened?" My voice trembled.

Bob gripped my shoulders. "Calm down," he said. "Cassie is all right. Let's talk about something else right now, okay? Don't you want to know how I proposed?"

"No. I need to see Cassie."

"I'll bring her here tomorrow, and you can see for yourself that she's fine, okay? You need to get a good night's rest, and when you wake up everything will be back to normal."

I doubted that. Waking up lately was more of a crap shoot than anything else. I had no idea what was normal anymore. I just knew I had to see Cassie with my own eyes to be sure she was okay.

"Please, Bob. I can't stand not knowing."

He sighed. I could see the moment he gave in to my demands. "Okay, but promise me that you'll try to get some rest afterward?"

I nodded.

"Okay, like I said, it was the day of Diane's wedding. You didn't want to leave Cassie alone, but she convinced you she'd be fine."

Yes, so far that was exactly how I remembered, except in my memory I hadn't been convinced. I'd stayed home with Cassie. Perhaps I'd simply used Cassie as an excuse to avoid having to pretend to be happy for a few hours.

"So you did the right thing by your friend, even though your instincts were telling you to stay home with your sister." Bob leaned back in his chair. "But Cassie was young and stubborn. When her friends called later that day, she decided she felt good enough to go out and party with them."

I had a bad feeling about where this story was going.

"There was an accident," Bob said, confirming my fears. "The car went off the road and hit a tree. Two of Cassie's friends died. Cassie survived, but she needed years of physical therapy after the accident and still wears the scars from that day."

"Oh my God."

Bob gripped my hand and gave it a brief shake. "It wasn't your fault. Cassie has learned to live with her physical scars, but you can't get over the emotional scars you carry from leaving your sister alone that day. You couldn't forgive yourself. You've spent every day of your life since then trying to make it up to her, even though it wasn't your fault."

"But if I'd stayed home that night . . ."

"It's time to let go," Bob said. "Stop blaming yourself and move on with your life. You can't change the past."

I closed my eyes. Hadn't I just heard words to that effect? My father's wife had said pretty much the same thing to me yesterday . . . in another lifetime.

"Do you think you can rest now?" Bob asked.

"I think so," I said. It was a lie. I wouldn't be able to rest until I'd seen Cassie with my own two eyes, but I knew that Bob wouldn't let me leave the hospital yet. His protectiveness was touching, but my loyalties were to my sister, so I had no qualms about lying to him.

"I'm feeling tired," I said, feigning a yawn. "I think you're right. All I need is a good night's sleep and things will be better in the morning."

He looked relieved. "I'll stay here with you until you fall asleep."

I started to argue, but it was easier to simply lay back and pretend to fall asleep. He ran his hand through my hair in a soothing gesture, and soon I didn't have to pretend. I drifted dreamily, feeling safe and loved.

———————

It might have been minutes or hours later that I realized Bob had left and I was alone. Here was my chance to slip out of the hospital and find Cassie. I gathered my clothes from the small bedside dresser and changed out of the hospital gown. I couldn't find my purse, but I wasn't surprised. If Bob had brought me to the hospital, he'd have no reason to even think of grabbing my purse. But without it, how would I find Cassie? I didn't have car keys or money or any identification.

That didn't stop me, however. I was determined to find Cassie if I had to walk all over town to do it. No one noticed me as I slipped out of the room and down the hall. I walked right past the nurse's station without breaking stride.

And then I saw him.

I stopped in my tracks and stared at the doctor walking toward me. "Parker?"

My brother glanced at me with no sign of recognition. I stopped and grabbed his arm. "Parker? It's me, Jenna."

"I'm sorry," he said with honest concern. "You must have me confused with someone else."

I glanced at his name tag—*Daniel Cody, M.D.* Not Parker. I took a closer look. I'd only known my brother for a few days, but surely I couldn't be mistaken.

"I thought you were . . . you look just like . . ." Before I could make more of a fool of myself, I caught sight of another familiar figure striding down the hallway. Maya closed the distance between us, then took my arm and steered me away from the Parker lookalike.

"Maya? It is you, isn't it?"

"Of course it is, dear. Who did you think it was?"

"I don't know who anyone is anymore. That doctor back there. He's not Parker?"

"He is and he isn't." She guided me back to my room.

"Wait. I have to find Cassie."

"No, you don't, child. Your sister is fine. You've spent your entire life taking care of her, and now it's time to take care of yourself. Understand me?"

"But . . ."

"No buts." Her voice grew uncharacteristically stern. "You don't have time to wallow in self-pity. All the answers you need are here; it's only a matter of finding them."

Reluctantly I did as I was told, soothed by the familiar voice of someone I'd come to trust. I climbed into bed and pulled the crisp hospital sheet up under my chin. "This would be so much easier if you simply explained everything to me, you know."

Maya pulled a chair up to the side of the bed. "I could," she said. "But that would defeat the purpose."

I yawned, this time for real. "I have some ideas," I said. "Would you tell me if I was on the right track?"

"I won't have to." She brushed the hair from my forehead in a motherly gesture that made me melt into the pillows. "You'll know when you're on the right track." Her smile warmed me. "And you know what you have to do."

"Watch, listen, and learn, right?" Another yawn made my voice crack.

"That's right." She winked. "Might as well get to know that handsome husband of yours while you're at it."

The word "husband" pulled me up short again. I'd forgotten about Bob. *My husband.* As shocking as that was, it felt right. It was as if I'd known from the first time we'd met that we were meant for each other. Was that destiny? All I knew was that even in a world where we'd just missed meeting each other, fate had thrown us into one another's path again. And I knew with certainty that if we hadn't met at the House of Cry, we'd have run into each other again somewhere else down the line.

At least I hoped that was the case.

11

The hospital room was real. No matter how hard I tried to convince myself that yesterday had all been a dream, there was no disputing the reality of these somber hospital walls. Which meant the rest of it was also real. Remembering what Bob had told me about Cassie broke my heart all over again.

I was still puzzled about seeing Parker in the halls the previous night, however. Was it possible he was a doctor in this reality? But then why hadn't he recognized me? As usual, Maya had left me with more questions than answers. She seemed to be leading me down a path where I could draw my own conclusions. I had a feeling that the sooner I figured things out, the sooner I'd find myself back where I belonged.

I'd stayed awake half the night puzzling over possibilities. Right now my biggest clue was the way my life seemed to diverge at the point of Diane's wedding. In my world I had stayed home with Cassie that night. Consequently, I'd never met Bob. That had also been the end of my friendship with Diane. In this current timeline, however, not only had I gone to the wedding, but I'd met and married Bob. Unfortunately, my sister had paid the consequences for my actions.

It all boiled down to choices. The choice I had made that night—whether to stay or go—had led to two separate realities. It seemed pretty clear cut. But what about the last reality I'd experienced? What choice had my mother made that turned her from a fun-loving, well-balanced housewife to a depressed and suicidal poet? Those were answers I had yet to find. Maybe that's why I was here.

Using the pin that Parker had given me as a visual aid, I drew a fingertip from the central trunk up to the first fork in the branches. This was where the unknown event that changed my mother's life had occurred. On one side was the well-adjusted woman I'd just left behind, and on the other was the suicidal mother of my memory.

I followed the path to the next juncture that I was aware of— Diane's wedding. On the one side I had attended and met Bob, on the other I had stayed home with Cassie. Did every single choice lead to an alternate reality or only the big, life-changing ones? We make dozens of decisions each day. How many alternate realities are there? And if every choice exists simultaneously, then who is to say which one is right and which one is wrong?

I was still trying to wrap my mind around the concept when the sight of Bob walking into my room kicked my heart rate up a notch. "How are you feeling this morning?" he asked.

"Better." It was the truth. And seeing him there helped my mood more than I could imagine. I knew instinctively that he was someone I could count on to be there for me when I needed him. When he sat beside my bed and squeezed my hand, I squeezed back. It felt like this was the timeline I was meant to be in—a world where I'd met the man of my dreams and we'd built a meaningful life together. But could I choose this world at Cassie's expense? And if I didn't, could I truly be happy going back to my real world knowing what alternate possibilities existed?

Bob held out his hand, palm up. "Look what I found," he said, holding out a golden wedding band.

I took it and turned it over, noticing the inscription inside. *Everwhen.* Why did that sound so familiar? Where had I heard it before?

Bob came around and wrapped one arm around my shoulder. "That's the title of a poem you wrote for me after I proposed."

Really? How odd. I don't write poetry. But I knew better than to say that aloud.

"This was my mother's ring," Bob said. His arm tightened around my shoulders. "She would have loved you."

So Bob's mother was also dead. Maybe the fact that we were both motherless was the common factor that brought us together. I wondered if there was an alternate reality where Bob's mother was alive. Did he have a Maya as well? Did everyone?

Bob took the ring from my palm and slid it onto my finger. It was a perfect fit. I glanced at him, then away again. It pained me to see the love in his eyes. I didn't deserve it, and I couldn't get used to anyone looking at me that way. This world was only temporary. If I became too accustomed to feeling loved, it would hurt too much to lose it all over again.

"Are you sure you're okay?" he asked.

"Yes, I think so. But it's hard not remembering everything."

"The doctor said the condition is only temporary," he said. "If not, I'll simply have to convince you to fall in love with me all over again."

I smiled. I had no doubt he'd be able to do just that.

"There's the smile I fell in love with." He leaned in and brushed his lips over mine before I could pull away. Or maybe I didn't really want to. His lips were gentle rather than demanding, casual rather than passionate. It was sweet, and he had no way of knowing that as far as I was concerned, this was our very first kiss.

And like the ring, it was perfect.

"I talked to the doctor, and he said there was no reason you couldn't be released. As long as you're sure you're feeling better."

"I'll feel better when I'm in my own home." I hoped that was the case. At least I could use the concussion as an excuse if I couldn't navigate the unfamiliar surroundings. Being home would give me more opportunities to find answers.

But going home brought up a whole new set of problems. Would Bob expect me to sleep in the same bed? Of course he would. We were married. I shook my head. I'd worry about that when the time came. For now I just wanted to get out of there, and that meant putting on a good show.

"Yes. Take me home."

———————

Bob made sure I was settled in my room—*our* room. How strange it felt to know I'd be sharing a room and a bed with a man tonight. Not that I hadn't shared a bed with a man before, but this was different. This was a marriage bed, and Bob was expecting to share it with his wife, a woman he knew intimately on so many levels. How could I live up to those expectations?

I felt perfectly at home, not only in this room but in the entire house. For some reason I wasn't surprised to find myself again living in the House of Cry. It was like my soul wasn't content until it found its way back here.

This life, this house, and this man all felt like *home*. But how could I appreciate this new world when I was still mourning the last? As much as my soul yearned for everything this reality had to offer, I knew I wouldn't be happy until I found myself back where I'd started.

Once I was alone, I slipped out of bed and began searching for a diary or journal, anything that could provide some clues to this existence. Writing seemed to be part of my nature, no matter how hard I tried to deny it. It was the one constant that carried through each timeline.

It turned out that I was right. The journal was tucked into my bedside nightstand. I settled back in bed, preparing to read the story of my life. I felt slightly guilty going through someone else's personal journal. I couldn't wrap my head around the fact that I had written these words in another timeline that I was unaware of having lived. To me they were written by someone else who looked like me, sounded like me, but wasn't me at all.

The writer of this journal had an optimistic outlook on life, in contrast to my sharp-edged pessimism. She saw the silver linings where I only saw dark clouds. I worried about her naïveté. She seemed to be dancing with wild abandon, unaware that the floor beneath her feet was littered with land mines. I wanted to warn her, but what good would that do? Maybe if our roles were reversed she'd feel just as sorry for me and all my dark fears. Maybe she'd tell me to lighten up and enjoy each day as if it were my last.

I thumbed through the pages, rediscovering the moment I first fell in love with Bob, our first date, our first kiss. I learned that he always brought me pink carnations on special occasions. I read about vacations with friends, parties we'd attended, and holidays when our house was filled with laughter and joy. I relived the evening Bob proposed to me on a moonlit beach and felt myself falling in love with him all over again.

Then I came across the poem he had told me about that had inspired him to inscribe the word "everwhen" inside our wedding bands.

EVERWHEN

I loved you when you weren't mine
And found you in forever time
I'll stay today, tomorrow, then
I'll love you still for everwhen

It was sweet and corny and romantic—nothing like my mother's heartrending poems. There was a playfulness and a poignancy to it that made me smile. I'd spent my life avoiding the label of writer because it belonged to my mother. I'd been so concerned that I'd inherited her dark side that I never allowed myself to explore the lighter side of my own creativity. Perhaps there were stories inside me as well, and books that were meant to be written.

Books.

My stomach dropped. I suddenly realized why the inscription in the wedding band had sounded so familiar. In my mind's eye I could clearly see the title of the book Maya had been holding in the library—*Doorway to Everwhen.*

It wasn't a coincidence. Everything was connected. But which came first, the poem or the book? Or did they both exist concurrently? Did it even matter? I'd been given this opportunity to find answers to questions that had haunted my entire life and I didn't want to waste a single moment worrying about minutiae.

———————

I was so engrossed in the pages of the journal I barely registered the fact that I was no longer alone. I glanced up and saw Cassie standing in the doorway. *Cassie!* I gasped, jumped out of bed, and closed the distance between us. I wrapped my arms around her. "Oh, Cassie, I've missed you." I wanted to hold on to her and never let go.

She pulled away, as if uncomfortable with the physical contact. That was crazy, though. Cassie was a hugger. If anything, I was usually the first to pull away.

I studied her, getting my first look at the scars crisscrossing her beautiful face. Even though Bob had prepared me, the sight was shocking. The most severe scar ran from her hairline across her forehead, bisecting one eyebrow and barely missing her eye before disappearing below her cheekbone. The second ran vertically through her bottom lip at the two-thirds point, then across her chin and along her jaw line. It broke my heart to see her face disfigured in this way. But even more painful was what I saw in her eyes. My happy, carefree sister was now guarded. Her smile was the same, but I could see the difference that years of living with looks of pity had done to her. Maybe no one else would notice, but I did. The scars went far deeper than just her skin.

One single impulsive decision had changed her life completely. Did she blame me? From what Bob had told me, I blamed myself. But what I now realized was that it had been Cassie's choice to go out that night, not mine. I couldn't and shouldn't take responsibility for her actions.

I ran my fingers through her hair. "I love you, Cassie." I fought the impulse to say I was sorry. Sorry for leaving her all alonely. Sorry for not being there to stop her from making a mistake that would change the rest of her life. I was sure I'd said those words thousands of times already, and no amount of apology would change anything. I wished I could tell her there were unblemished versions of herself living in worlds where she didn't have to hide her face from cruel stares, but maybe that would only hurt her more.

She didn't respond at first. Then she replied in a soft, hesitant voice. "I love you too, Sis."

I held her close. I'd taken care of Cassie for as long as I remembered. Only now did I realize that a small part of me had also resented her, blaming her for the loss of my own childhood. It wasn't Cassie's fault that I'd had to take on an extra burden of responsibility. She hadn't put me in that position. Letting go of that resentment lifted an unseen weight from my heart. I thought I'd loved my sister as much as I could, but it was only a fraction of what I felt now.

Bob came into the room, breaking up the moment before it could become uncomfortable. "Can I get you girls something to drink?"

"Green tea," we replied at the same time. She smiled at me, and I smiled back. Then we both started laughing. For as long as

I could remember, we'd answered random questions in unison. There was comfort in knowing that some things never changed.

And just like that we were on familiar ground.

The three of us spent the next few hours talking over tea and pound cake at the kitchen table. I tried not to act surprised when Cassie complimented me on the cake. It was very good. I'd have to give myself the recipe.

When Bob left us alone, I leaned close and whispered to Cassie. "I need to talk to Dad. Would you come with me?" I knew I was taking a chance, but I could always pull out the "head injury" card if I had to.

As it turned out, that wasn't necessary. "Sure," she said. "When?"

I glanced in the other room, where Bob had disappeared. He'd been hovering over me since we'd arrived home. I was sure he'd veto the idea of me leaving today. "How about tomorrow?" I asked. That would give me time to convince Bob that I was well enough to be out of his sight for a few hours.

Cassie picked up her cup and placed it in the sink, then came back and gave me a brief hug. "I'll pick you up about noon tomorrow," she said. "He shouldn't be too drunk that early. If he is, we can go to lunch so it won't be a total bust."

Drunk? It sounded like my father's behavior in this timeline was more similar to the one I remembered—unlike the last reality, where he'd found redemption with a new wife and family. Nothing was perfect, no matter which path I followed.

Bob showed Cassie out. They had a whispered exchange at the door that I was sure had to do with me, but I was beyond caring if my behavior was suspicious or not. If everything went right, tomorrow Cassie and I would get the answers we should have been given years ago. And just maybe those answers would put me on the path back to the world where I belonged.

Bob came up behind me and put his arms around my shoulders. He leaned down and brushed his lips across my jaw line. "It was nice seeing the two of you so comfortable together." His voice sent delicious shivers down my spine. Maybe sharing a bed wasn't such a bad idea. After all, we *were* married.

"Know what I'd like to do tonight?"

I was almost afraid to ask, considering where my mind had just ventured. "What's that?"

"I'd like to take my girl to dinner at our favorite restaurant, then dance with her under the moonlight."

"Sounds like fun," I said. "Can I come too?"

He chuckled, and the sound triggered a wave of laughter that started deep in my belly, expanded into my chest, then erupted from my lips. It had been so long since I'd laughed with such unbridled joy that I almost didn't recognize the sound.

I turned, then stopped when I noticed a familiar cabinet in the corner. "Is this . . . ?"

"Your mother's old record player," he said.

I crossed the room and ran my hands over the polished wood surface of the vintage cabinet. "She never called it a record player," I said. "It was always her *Victrola.*"

Bob came beside me as I opened the lid, revealing the turntable. "This must be worth a fortune." Not that I'd ever sell it in a million years. I didn't remember what had happened to this record player in my own world, but seeing it now triggered distant memories and filled me with a yearning desire.

"Look," I said. "Real vinyl records! Do you have any idea how hard it is to find these?"

"Not when you work at a record store," he replied, searching my face for what I could only assume were signs of remembrance.

I didn't remember but wasn't surprised by this revelation. Besides the journals, music seemed to be another constant thread that wove through all of my realities. I opened another cabinet drawer and found stacks of records exactly where I remembered them being kept when I was a little girl. I sat cross-legged on the floor and separated them into piles, old and new. As I revealed one yellowed record sleeve after another, I could hear the old, familiar songs in my head. Lyrics that tugged at your heartstrings. Songs that made you sway to the melody. Music that made you *feel.*

No wonder I'd strayed so far in the other direction musically. Feeling was difficult. It stripped naked emotions that could break your heart. These old songs carried memories that were better left forgotten. Or were they? Maybe it was time to stop blotting out those memories with noise and chaos. Maybe it was time to remember the things that weren't painful and forgive the ones that were.

Bob leaned over and kissed the top of my head. "I'll go make reservations for tonight," he said. "You have some time to go through these records."

And I did, listening to one after the other. Sometimes putting a record back on the turntable and playing it again just for the sheer pleasure of it. I didn't even realize I was crying until my tears splattered on the dust jacket of an old Beatles album. But they were good tears. Healing tears.

When Bob came back, I had separated all the albums and records into piles: sentimental, dance music, torch songs, classics, and rock. "These records," I pointed out, "are just silly. I can't believe the nonsense lyrics. *I am the eggman? Someone left a cake out in the rain?* I could write better lyrics than that."

"I'm sure you could," Bob agreed."

"Music should raise you up to a higher level," I said. "Make you feel something."

"Have you thought about it?" Bob asked.

"Thought about what?"

"Writing songs?" His eyes searched mine. Was this something we'd discussed before? Did I have dreams of catching my big break in this lifetime as well as the last?

"My mother's the writer." The words came automatically, as if denying any resemblance to her made me saner somehow. But that was the old me. Now I understood her better. I could admit that sharing her talent didn't mean I was destined for the same end.

Suddenly it felt right. Not just writing in my journal or writing poems like my mother did, but combining writing with this passion for music. I could write songs that healed the body and soothed the soul.

Bob took my hand and lifted me to my feet. "Enough records for now. I've made reservations at your favorite restaurant, and you only have two hours to get ready." He smiled like this was a private joke between the two of us.

I only wished I remembered the punch line.

12

Bob was right. The Warwick really was my favorite restaurant. It was an out-of-the-way little jewel of a place with a hearty but reasonably priced menu. I came here often to eat, usually choosing a quiet spot on the deck overlooking the lake. I had no memory of being here with Bob, however. I usually came by myself with only a book as my dinner companion. Now that I thought about it, I always had a book tucked into my purse in case I had to wait in line or spend time alone. Books were good company. Plus they made effective barriers. People rarely approached someone engrossed in a book.

The hostess greeted us by name. We stopped three times on the way to our table to talk to people who seemed happy to see us. It was a little overwhelming having to keep my happy face on for people I didn't know, but I didn't want to embarrass Bob. There'd be no hiding behind the pages of a book tonight.

"Do we know everyone in town?" I asked, only half joking.

"Pretty much," he replied, pulling out my chair when we finally reached our table. "What can I say, people gravitate to you. I'm just along for the ride."

"That's so not like me," I mumbled.

"What?"

"Nothing." I ordered a glass of wine while I studied the menu, trying to decide between panko-crusted salmon on wilted greens or one of the Italian specialties the restaurant was famous for. "I think I'll have the eggplant Parmesan tonight," I said.

Bob wasn't listening. I saw him gesturing to someone behind me. I turned and gaped when I saw Diane walking toward us. It wasn't the sight of her that surprised me. I assumed we'd still be friends in this lifetime since I'd met Bob at her wedding. I also figured we'd most likely run into each other again. What caught me off guard was the high round belly that cleared a path before her. She looked about fourteen months pregnant.

I stood and held my arms out, gathering her close in a genuine and heartfelt hug. "Look at you. You're positively glowing."

"Yeah, I'm a great big glowing hippo."

"Stop it. You look gorgeous."

Her husband, who'd been walking slightly behind, pressed a kiss to her cheek. "I couldn't agree more."

Bob pulled out a chair for Diane. "Why don't you two join us?"

Diane lowered herself carefully onto the straight-backed chair, leaning back to balance her weight. "Only if you let me sniff your wine."

"One sniff, then you're cut off," I said with a chuckle."

"Story of my life." She gave her swollen belly a slow, tender caress. The Madonna-like smile on her face made it hard to take her complaints seriously. "Guess who the final two contenders for godparents are?" she asked.

"Contenders?" Bob pretended outrage. "I thought we were the only ones in the running."

"That could be why you made it to the finals."

Bob turned to Diane's husband. "Are you going to let her get away with that, Dean?"

Dean! That was his name. I wondered if Bob had made a point of using it to help jog my memory. If so, I was grateful. Forgetting the daddy's name would have surely taken us out of the running as godparents.

The good-natured banter continued throughout dinner. I tried to take a mental picture of this moment. I wanted to remember it forever, pulling it up like a worn photograph to savor when I was feeling lonely. The sun was just beginning to set, turning the sky into a pastel parfait and sending glittering reflections across the water's surface. Candlelight softened the features of everyone around the table and made their eyes sparkle with merriment. It felt like family.

Bob leaned close. "Hear that?"

I gave a slight shake to my head. "What?"

"They're playing our song." He stood up and took my hand. "Care to dance?"

He led me to the small dance floor, where I moved easily into his arms. I recognized the song playing: "A Thousand Nights," a soft, seductive song filled with yearning. Our song? I'd never had a song before, but this one felt perfect.

Bob drew me so close I could feel his heartbeat. I swayed against him, feeling the sexual heat of his body against mine. Passion simmered low and deep, spreading upward in slow, steady waves. I closed my eyes and let the music seduce me.

A lifetime is too brief,
An eternity too short,
But I'll start with a thousand days,
And a thousand nights of you

The song ended far too soon. I didn't want the night to end. I was so comfortable and relaxed with Bob, Diane, and Dean. This was the life I should have had: friends who meant the world to me and a husband I adored. It was my own fault I didn't have these things in my real life. I'd never learned to love myself enough to let other people close. No wonder I was all alone. I hoped it wasn't too late to change, because a part of me knew this was only temporary.

I would have loved to accept everything Bob had to offer— unconditional love and support. I wanted to wallow in it, bathe in it, and lose myself forever. But I knew my time here was limited. And even more than the last time, it would kill me to leave this behind. I'd never get to hold Diane's child or grow old with Bob. I'd go through my entire life wondering who was loving him in my place.

But I couldn't stay. This life didn't belong to me. The one I needed to return to was out there somewhere. It might not be perfect, but it was the life I was familiar with. And now that I knew what kinds of possibilities existed, I could take steps to move in the right direction. I couldn't bring my mother back, but there was peace in knowing that we never really lose the people we love. They're simply moving along different paths.

What about Bob? Why did we keep crossing paths? Were we meant to be together? Had I promised myself to him in another lifetime? It broke my heart, because I felt myself falling in love with him. Already I couldn't imagine a life without Bob in it. I wanted this life, the house and home and future children. I wanted to grow old with him.

I wondered in how many lifetimes I'd already fallen in love with Bob and how often we'd just missed meeting each other by seconds or hours or days. I knew one thing for sure. If and when I got back to my real world, one of the first things I was going to do was find Bob and convince him that we were meant to be together. Even if it meant putting myself out there to be hurt. I wouldn't know until I tried. I couldn't bear to waste another moment waiting for my soul mate to arrive when I already knew his name.

A haunting melody ran through my head, remnants of one of the old records I'd played that afternoon. The words had tugged at my heart then and were even more bittersweet now. *When I'm alone with only dreams of you, that won't come true, what'll I do.*

I reached out and grasped Bob's hand.

He leaned close and whispered, "Are you all right?"

I nodded, blinking away the tears in my eyes. "I'm just happy," I said.

And that was the absolute truth.

It was too early to go to bed when we came home from the restaurant, and I still wasn't sure how to approach Bob about our sleeping arrangements.

"Do you want to talk more?" he asked. "I mean, you know, go over things you don't remember?"

"Actually, I'm feeling a bit of information overload. Would you mind if I took a bath before turning in for the night?" I did my best thinking in the bathtub, and it would give me some time to decompress. Plus it would give me a chance to search the house for the secret room. Maybe my time here would be short and sweet. I was worried that if I stayed here too long, I'd never want to leave.

Bob reached for the remote control, then sprawled on the couch. "Take your time," he said. "There's a movie I wanted to watch tonight anyway. Unless you need me to . . ."

I held up my hand before he could get to his feet again. "I'm sure I can manage." How hard could it be to find bubble bath and a towel? "I'm just going to take a look around, too. See if something might jog my memory."

Bob glanced up from his channel surfing. "Okay. Let me know if you need anything."

I left him on the couch and went searching through the house. I should have felt like a trespasser, but I didn't. I could see my personal touch everywhere, from the color palette to the furnishings to the smallest knickknack. I couldn't have felt more at home if I'd decorated it myself. Which I obviously had.

I opened doors, more relieved than disappointed when I didn't encounter the secret room. If I had to be trapped in an alternate life, this was the one I'd choose. I shook my head. No, I couldn't let myself get too comfortable here. No matter how much I wanted it to be, this wasn't my real home.

After checking every room in the house, I made my way back to the bathroom. I found a jar of lavender bath crystals beside the bathtub. I adjusted the spray until it was just the right temperature, then poured a generous handful of the bath crystals under the running water. Feeling a bit self-conscious, I turned the lock on the bathroom door before undressing. It was silly. Obviously Bob had seen me naked on plenty of occasions, but I wasn't quite ready for that level of intimacy yet. I sank into the tub with a deep sigh and felt the tension ease from my muscles.

I closed my eyes and went over the day. I'd spent most of my time frantically searching for clues. It was exhausting and frustrating but better than the lifeless lethargy I'd become accustomed to. For such a long time I'd been numb, living life on the sidelines. I'd prided myself on keeping my emotions in check. Now, as frustrating as it was, I felt alive for the first time in a long time. Life had new meaning, and the future was one of limitless possibilities. It was time I stepped off the sidelines and took control of my own life.

I sank deeper into the tub, luxuriating in the aromatic warmth. My body felt limp and relaxed, as opposed to the tightly strung tension I was accustomed to. It almost felt as if I'd slipped into someone else's body. Why not? I was living someone else's life, enjoying someone else's lavender bath crystals, and yes, loving someone else's husband. Even though that someone was another version of myself and it was beyond my control, I still felt like a thief.

When the water had grown cool and I could no longer avoid facing reality, I stepped out of the tub and dried off. Since I hadn't thought to bring clean clothes in with me and couldn't bear the thought of getting back into the clothes I'd worn all night, I helped myself to the bathrobe I found hanging from a hook inside the door. It was soft and fluffy and comfortably worn in. That seemed symbolic of the rest of this life. Warm and comfortable but not mine.

I came out of the bathroom and caught Bob carrying pillows and a blanket to the couch.

"Where are you going?"

He colored sheepishly. "I thought, you know, seeing as how you can't remember and all, that maybe you'd like your privacy for a little while."

If I hadn't already been falling in love with him, that chivalrous act alone would have done it.

"You don't even remember our wedding day," he said. "I'd feel like a molester climbing into bed with you."

"We didn't sleep together before we were married?" I asked coyly.

He raised an eyebrow. "The fact that you can't remember is another argument in favor of me sleeping on the couch tonight."

"Can I be honest with you?"

"Absolutely."

"I appreciate your gallantry more than you know. But the truth is, I don't want to be alone tonight."

He let out a long sigh. "Neither do I," he said.

"Good." I pulled the robe a little tighter around myself. "Then why don't you tell me what I usually wear to bed?"

"Nothing," he said, avoiding my shocked expression. He put the blankets back in the closet and pulled out a cotton nightgown. "Nothing except for this," he said with a sly chuckle.

I punched his shoulder, then took the nightgown. "Do I usually think you're funny?"

"All the time."

He turned and walked out of the room. "I'll be back in ten minutes," he called over his shoulder. "Make sure you're decent."

I laughed but waited until I was sure I was alone before changing into the nightgown. I sat on the side of the bed and stared at the wedding ring on my finger for a few moments, then climbed under the covers with my back to the door.

I didn't turn when Bob came back in the room, or when the mattress dipped and I felt the heat of his body against my back.

I stayed perfectly still, even when his arm came around my waist and his lips pressed against the pulse right below my ear. "Good-night, sweetheart," he whispered.

I felt a slow shiver deep inside me. "'Night," I murmured back, snuggling against the curve of his body. We fit perfectly together. Feeling safe and secure, I drifted effortlessly into a deep and dreamless sleep.

13

I woke to the smell of sizzling bacon. I drew the aroma deep into my lungs, stretched, and greeted the new day with a smile. I wondered if Bob usually rose before I did, or whether he'd purposely given me time alone this morning to avoid any awkwardness. I appreciated the thought but honestly didn't feel awkward at all. In fact, I was a bit disappointed not to wake up pressed against his warm, hard body. Who knew where that might have led?

Oh, who was I kidding? I knew exactly where I wanted it to lead. Every nerve in my body tingled with anticipation. I wanted to seduce my husband. I wanted to make wild and crazy love to him, but it looked like I might have to settle for bacon instead.

I climbed out of bed and made my way to the bathroom. A glance in the mirror caught me by surprise. Who was this smiling woman with the glowing skin? I ran a brush through my hair, marveling at the shine. Is this what contentment did to a person? If so, it was better than Botox.

I changed into a pair of soft, worn-in jeans and a royal-blue tank top. The clothes fit me perfectly, which shouldn't have surprised me, but it did. What especially surprised me, however, was a small tattoo on my inner left forearm. I studied it closely. It was a delicate white swan. I rubbed my skin gently just to be sure it was permanent.

How odd. I'd never been adventurous in any way. The only things pierced were my ears, and up until now there had been no ink anywhere on my body. I made a mental note to ask Bob what significance it held.

I made my way downstairs and watched Bob from the kitchen doorway. He looked even more appealing in the morning. His hair was slightly mussed, as if he'd just run his fingers through it after climbing out of bed. The gray T-shirt he wore looked soft and well worn. I made up my mind to steal it at the first available opportunity so I could surround myself with his scent. He tossed a sizzling pan of home fries with the finesse of a master chef. There is something incredibly sexy about a man who knows his way around a kitchen.

I cleared my throat, and he turned with a smile. "Morning, gorgeous."

Who, me?

"I wasn't sure if you wanted French toast or chocolate chip pancakes and I didn't want to wake you up, so I made an executive decision and went with the pancakes."

"Perfect choice," I said. I didn't even know I liked chocolate chip pancakes until just this moment, but suddenly that was exactly what I wanted.

He motioned me to a small bistro-style table already set with plates, linen napkins, and a crystal decanter of chilled orange juice. In the center of the table was a bud vase holding a single pink carnation. I remembered reading in the journal that pink carnations were something special between them . . . between us. I sat while Bob brought breakfast to the table. I could certainly become accustomed to this.

"May I ask you a question?"

He pulled up a chair beside me. "Of course. You can ask me anything."

I held out my arm. "When did I get this?"

"Ahhh, your animal totem?"

I frowned. "My what?"

"You always said the swan represented every aspect of your life that you wanted to work on. The 'S' stands for spiritual growth, the 'W' for work ethic, the 'A' for acceptance, and the 'N' for nutritional health. You said if you spent part of each day attending to each of those four areas of your life, you could transform from an ugly duckling to a swan."

"Wow."

"I never understood it myself," he said. "To me you've always been a beautiful swan."

"Awww." I traced my fingers over the tattoo—spirit, work, acceptance, and nutrition. It felt right. "I love it!"

"Of course you do," he said with a quirky grin. "It was your idea."

I dug into my pancakes as if I hadn't eaten in years. They were light and fluffy and delicious. I glanced up and saw Bob watching me. He smiled, but not before I caught the guarded expression in his eyes. Did he know I was an imposter wearing his wife's clothes? I reached across the table for a slice of bacon, but he caught my wrist and stopped me.

"You're a vegetarian," he said.

"Oh? You didn't say anything at the restaurant last night."

"Why would I? You ordered eggplant. I didn't think anything of it." He snatched a slice of bacon and crunched down on it.

"But you eat meat?"

"It's one of my many faults. Lucky for me, you love me in spite of them all."

I seriously doubted he had any faults to speak of. Differences maybe, but isn't that what made life interesting? I tried not to think about bacon. It was important to me to honor the body I temporarily inhabited. Unless, of course, that included yoga. In that case, it was on its own, swan or no swan.

I glanced again at the pile of bacon. If he was the only one eating it, why had he made so much? My question was answered when Cassie barreled through the door, mumbled something that almost sounded like "Morning," then swept past the table, grabbed a slice of bacon, and stuffed the entire thing in her mouth.

"Help yourself," I said, watching her chomp on the bacon with more than a little envy.

"I have to," she replied. "Ever since you became a vegetarian, I've had to help poor Bob eat your share of breakfast meat. He can't figure out how to cook bacon for one."

I washed down my grumpiness with a swig of coffee. Thank goodness I still had that. I glanced at Bob, just in case, but saw no sign that I'd given up caffeine as well.

"So," Cassie said. "Are you up for a visit with Dad this morning?"

Something in the tone of her voice sent up a red flag. "Sure," I said hesitantly. "Why not?"

Cassie shot a glance at Bob. "Well, the last time you talked to him you two had an argument."

"About what?"

Cassie looked down, then up again. "Just stuff," she said. "Stuff that happened a long time ago."

I had a feeling that some of it might be related to what happened to Cassie. I know that for a long time I resented my father's absences. He shouldn't have placed so much responsibility on my shoulders. Maybe if he'd been around, things would have been different. Was that it? Did I blame him for what happened to Cassie that night? Maybe it was easier than carrying all of the guilt on my own shoulders.

I shook my head. It didn't matter. He was the only living link to my mother's past. If I was going to find clues to the life I came from, I had to start by talking to him. "I'm ready if you are," I told Cassie.

She snatched another piece of bacon for the road. "Let's go now then, before he has his second round of boilermakers." She glanced at her watch. "If we wait until noon he'll be half in the bag."

It was mildly reassuring to know that some things never changed. I knew from past experience that there was no reasoning with my father when he was drunk. If Cassie was right, then we shouldn't waste another minute.

_____

My father seemed to have aged twenty years since I'd last seen him. His face was drawn in downward lines, and his grizzled chin was speckled with salt-and-pepper whiskers. He seemed sad and vulnerable. I wanted to hug him, despite our differences. He wasn't perfect. None of us is. But maybe he'd done the best he could. Maybe he drank to blot out his own regrets.

He held my gaze with a hard-eyed stare. "You look different," he said.

Odd that he'd be the one to see through my disguise. "I changed my hair," I said.

He frowned, then looked away. Either I was a convincing liar or he didn't really care one way or the other. My relationship with my father had always been strained, even before my mother's death. It seemed like this life was no different.

Cassie came around and gave him a peck on the cheek that looked more like obligation than affection. She dropped into a muddy-green armchair covered with dark stains. The arms were worn down to the cotton batting, and it let out an ominous creak when she settled into the cushion. I looked around for something less repulsive to sit on and settled on a metal folding chair. I followed Cassie's gaze to the half-full shot glass and beer bottle on the side table. It was ten o'clock.

I thought back to the last time I'd tried to visit my father, to the neat little house and manicured yard littered with little-boy toys. I remembered the protective wife who'd stood guard between my father and me just a few days ago. The comparison made his present state even more depressing.

I decided to get right to the point. "Dad, I need to find out more about what happened to Mom."

He let out a long, drawn-out sigh. "Why dredge all that up again?"

"Because it's important to me," I said. "All these years I've wor-ried that I'd inherited whatever weakness caused her to take her own life. I keep thinking I'll do the same thing."

He shook his head. "No, your mother's problems weren't genetic."

"How do you know?"

"I just do," he said, avoiding my gaze. I knew he was hiding something. His shoulders were hunched in a defensive posture, his lips clamped tight together.

I'd heard all the whispers and innuendo about my mother's state of mind, her depression, the dark strain that ran through all of her writing. But there had to be more to it. The mother I'd just left was as far away from the suicidal mother of my memory as she could be. So what had changed?

There was only one thing I could think of: Parker. Taking a deep breath, I decided to take a chance and ask the obvious ques-tion. "Did Mom have a son before I was born?"

My father's shoulders sagged in resignation. He sank onto the couch, his eyes looking everywhere but at Cassie and me. "I kept hoping this day would never come. Guess it was only a matter of time before you found out."

Cassie's eyes widened. She looked at me questioningly, but I just shook my head. I felt guilty for not warning her in advance, but it was important that we both hear my father's story at the same time.

He reached for the whiskey and swallowed it in one long gulp. "Your mother and I were engaged when I went in the service," he said hesitantly. "I went off to war, and when I came back ten months later she was pregnant." He rolled one shoulder and shook his head. "Obviously it wasn't mine."

He wouldn't meet my eyes. One fingertip traced lazy figure eights in the ring left on the table from his beer bottle. "I blame myself," he said. "If I hadn't made her choose . . ."

The import of what he was saying had barely sunk in when Cassie spoke up. "You made her choose between you and her baby?"

He nodded. "I was so full of anger. I couldn't look at the boy without feeling betrayed. He was a painful reminder of how your mother cheated on me while I was overseas fighting a senseless war."

Cassie's voice was a whisper. "He was just a baby."

"I know. And you can't imagine how many times I wished I'd been more tolerant. But I was just a kid myself. A kid who'd grown up too fast in the front line of a foreign country. I only cared about myself, not what it would do to your mother." He exhaled and seemed to shrink before my eyes. "The war broke my spirit, but your mother broke my heart."

I thought about the grown-up brother I'd met in a world where my mother had made a different choice. Things were beginning to fall into place.

"For a while it looked like everything would be okay," my father said. "She got pregnant almost immediately with you, Jenna. I thought another baby—my baby—would take away some of the pain. But it only made things worse. She became obsessed with finding out what had happened to her son, but the adoption agency wouldn't tell her anything. She walked all over town looking for children of the same age, the same complexion and hair color. She'd stop strangers on the street and ask about their child's birth date. She couldn't let it go."

Cassie stood up and started pacing, but our father seemed not to notice.

"I thought maybe if I gave her a son . . ." His voice trailed off.

Cassie stopped and stared, realizing what he was referring to. "Sorry to disappoint you," she said. The bitterness in her voice broke my heart.

He glanced at her, then away again. He continued speaking, more to himself than to us, it seemed. "After Cassie was born, she had complications and couldn't have another child. It didn't really matter. All the children in the world couldn't make up for the one she'd lost." He shrugged his shoulders. "That's when she started drinking to try to ease the depression. I guess I started drinking then, too. It was the only thing we had in common anymore."

He reached for the shot glass, found it empty, and pulled his hand back. "One day she read a newspaper account of a little boy who'd been beaten and killed by his foster parents. She was convinced it was the son she'd given away. She had no proof, but the ages were the same and the boy had the same hair and eye color, even the same birthday." He shook his head. "I tried to tell her that there were probably hundreds of kids born on that day, but it didn't help."

I could have told him he was right. I knew that Parker was alive. I'd seen him at the hospital just the other night. He had a different name and a different profession, but I knew it was him.

"Your mother was convinced it was her son," he continued. "Social Services wouldn't answer her questions, and the guilt and self-hatred ate away at her. She became more and more depressed. After that, she couldn't even look at either one of you without feeling shame and guilt. Her poetry became darker and more desperate. And finally . . ."

I knew how it ended. My mother simply couldn't live with the choice she'd made. Now I knew where the split occurred. On one side my mother chose her son, raised Parker, and lived a happy and fulfilling life. On the other side, she chose her husband over her child and paid the price with her own sanity.

"It wasn't the first time she had tried," he said. His eyes, rheumy with liquor, grief, or guilt, shifted from me to Cassie and back again. "Each time she failed, she learned how to do it better. The pull to die was greater than her will to live."

For a brief moment my father's eyes darkened with sober clarity. "Such a waste," he murmured. "She was so talented, so brilliant. I always wondered what her life would have been like if I hadn't forced her to choose."

I could have told him. I could have painted a picture of a woman living a life without regrets, a life where guilt wasn't eating her from the inside out, sharp teeth ripping her heart open a little bit at a time. But what good would that do?

Beside me, I heard a pitiful sob escape from Cassie's mouth. She stood and faced our father, her entire body trembling. Tears shimmered in her eyes. "So you're saying I was just an afterthought? I was conceived as a Band-Aid to fix Mom's broken heart, huh? And I didn't even do that right? I could never be the son she'd lost."

Dad's eyes widened in shock, as if she'd slapped him. "I didn't say that, Cass."

He hadn't said it, but he'd implied as much. No wonder Cassie was upset. Her voice trembled with anger. "How dare you! First your selfishness takes our mother away, then you leave us to practically raise ourselves, and now we find out we have a brother you couldn't bother telling us about? How dare you keep that a secret?"

He seemed stunned by her outburst. "I expect that from your sister," he said with a glance in my direction. "But not from you." He reached out for Cassie, but she turned away.

I was just as stunned by Cassie's outburst. Apparently I didn't have the market cornered on resentment. How long had this anger been simmering beneath the surface? Had I been too self-absorbed in my own misery to notice?

I couldn't count the number of times Cassie had laughingly called me the Patron Saint of Self-Righteous Misery. Maybe she felt I was sullen enough for both of us, and she was obligated to be the cheerful, optimistic one, the yin to my yang. I wondered which was worse, me wearing my depression like a cloak or Cassie burying it deep inside until it erupted like an infected abscess.

Cassie whipped around and stormed out. With only a single look back at my father, I turned and followed Cassie out the door. He'd had a lifetime to live with his own regrets. For Cassie, it was brand new. She needed me more than he did right now. I rushed to keep up with her.

"How long have you known?" Cassie asked, climbing into her car.

"I wasn't sure," I said. That was mostly the truth. The sister Cassie knew had no way of knowing about Parker. And even though I'd met him just a few days ago, I hadn't put it all together. I couldn't have known how much his birth had impacted our mother's life, and our lives as well.

"We have to find him," she said.

I nodded, joining her inside the car. Neither of us spoke for a long time, each lost in our own thoughts. I could only imagine what Cassie was thinking. For myself, I worried that perhaps I'd made a mistake. Maybe I'd set in motion a series of events that had no business existing in this timeline.

"Ten little fingers," Cassie whispered.

A chill ran down my spine at the familiar words. They were indelibly printed on my memory even though I hadn't heard them aloud in over twenty years. I remembered my mother walking the halls late at night with all the lights off, her voice a whispered monotone as she repeated the rhyme.

> *Ten little fingers*
> *Ten little toes*
> *Hazel eyes and a button nose*
> *Where did you come from?*
> *Where did you go?*
> *Ten little fingers*
> *Ten little toes*

Not a nursery rhyme, as I'd thought all those years ago, but a haunting requiem. It was the epitaph my mother had carved on the stone monument of her heart, written for the child she'd lost.

A few days ago I might not have understood the extent of my mother's feelings of pain and loss, but now that I'd spent the last few days in a world where Cassie was missing, I had a better understanding. I would have done anything to find my way back to her. How much more would my mother have grieved over the loss of a child she'd given birth to, nursed, and loved? Add to that the guilt of choosing her husband over her child and it was a toxic brew, poisoning her slowly and painfully day by day until the only escape was death.

We drove past the cemetery, and I glanced automatically in the direction of my mother's grave, barely visible from the road. There was a figure standing in the shadows. As if feeling my gaze on her, the figure turned. Even from a distance I recognized that profile. *Maya?*

My pulse racing, I grabbed Cassie's arm. "Stop the car!"

"What? Why?"

"There's someone at Mom's grave. Pull over."

"There's always someone there," she said. But she pulled over just the same. "You'd think after all these years the death groupies would stop haunting Mom's grave."

I jumped out of the car and ran through the cemetery. When I reached the spot where my mother's headstone was, however, there was no sign of Maya.

The sight of my mother's grave hit me hard. Before it was just a plot of earth littered with the sorrow of others, a place where I could feed my anger and resentment. Now, however, I had two mothers to mourn—the one I'd lost years ago and the new and improved version I'd lost only yesterday.

I wished I'd taken advantage of my time with her. There were things I should have said, words that could never be spoken now.

I wished I'd encouraged her to take up writing again, because her talent deserved a voice. I should have gotten to know Parker better, too, before he was lost to me.

And what about this new life I found myself in? Would I ever find my way back, or was I destined to spend the rest of my life wandering, a constant visitor haunting alternate versions of myself? And if I did find my way home, would I return with a newfound contentment or fall back into the same self-defeating behavior?

Maya would know. Had I simply imagined seeing her? Or was it wishful thinking? Then I noticed the open book lying face down on my mother's grave. I saw the title and knew I hadn't been mistaken.

Doorway to Everwhen. I picked it up and found a sheet of paper beneath it. Another of my mother's poems, torn from the pages of a book and left by some hopeless soul at my mother's grave.

> *grief is like a feather*
> *drifting slowly to the*
> *deepest*
> *blackest*
> *bottomless*
> *depths of my heart*
> *strangling*
> *choking*
> *chipping away at my soul*
> *and not even the hottest tears*
> *can wash away the sorrow*

Tears fell freely from my eyes. I wanted to go back and hold the woman I'd only now gotten to know. I wanted to somehow ease the pain and tell her there were worlds where the sorrow couldn't reach her, worlds where she remained unbroken.

I thought of the birthday cake we'd shared just days ago, the night when we'd watched movies and laughed together, the photographs that had sent her memory back over the years of a lifetime spent doing exactly what she loved most.

I reached out and brushed my fingers over the cool marble stone. "It's okay, Mom. I understand. I love you and I forgive you." The words were like a balm, healing a wound deep inside me.

I leaned back on my heels and turned my attention to the book. I riffled through the pages, seeing the notes Maya had scribbled inside when we had sat together in the library. She *had* been here. I'd have loved to sit down and talk to Maya about the ideas that were starting to come together in my mind, but I had a feeling I'd have to make do with this book for the time being.

14

A gentle hand brushed my shoulder. "Are you okay?"

Cassie. A feeling of déjà vu rushed over me. Had it only been a few days ago when my sister found me standing in this very same spot? It seemed so close and yet so far away, as if I'd lived a lifetime of experiences since we'd left this cemetery and first entered the House of Cry.

I couldn't help but reflect on my state of mind that morning. I'd been teetering on the razor's edge, ready to give up the life I had. Now I'd give anything to have it back, especially knowing what I knew now.

All my life I'd worried about inheriting my mother's suicidal tendencies, but my fears were unfounded. It wasn't genetic. There was no faulty suicide gene lurking inside me and waiting to seal my fate. And to think that one morning I'd almost surrendered to that dark cloud of depression.

"Yeah, I'm okay," I said. And I was. A weight had lifted from my shoulders. I no longer felt doomed to carry on in my mother's footsteps. There was a reason my mother couldn't break out of her own depression. Suicide was her choice, not my legacy.

Cassie knelt down at the foot of our mother's grave. "You want to know how stupid I was?" she asked. "All these years I blamed myself. I thought maybe if I'd been more polite or kept my room cleaner, said please and thank you." She took a deep, trembling breath. "I thought maybe I wasn't good enough or smart enough or pretty enough. I thought maybe if I were, she wouldn't have . . ." Her voice broke. "Wouldn't have left us."

"Oh, Cassie." I knelt beside her and wrapped my arms around her shoulders. A chill breeze sent a shiver through my body. For a moment I wondered if my mother's ghost had passed by us. "I thought that way myself sometimes."

"But it wasn't true," she said bitterly. "She didn't think about me at all one way or the other. I was just an attempt to replace the son she'd lost. When that failed, she didn't give me another thought. I certainly wasn't important enough to be a reason to live."

"You can't blame yourself, Cassie."

"Oh, I don't." she said, and there was a new steel in her voice. "I don't blame myself at all. Not anymore."

Her eyes narrowed, and what I saw in them sent a shiver down my spine.

"I blame him," she said, obviously referring to our father.

I fully understood her anger, but if there was one thing I'd learned over these last few days, it was the futility of placing blame on anyone. "It was her choice," I said with a longing glance at my mother's headstone. "She could have stood up to him and chosen to keep the baby."

And if she had, Cassie wouldn't be here. I knew the truth. In another reality our mother had made that choice. Dad had tried to live with her decision, at least up until my birth. Ultimately he'd given up on their marriage and moved on long before Cassie would have been conceived. I couldn't tell her that, however.

We swayed side by side for a long time, each of us trapped in our own thoughts. I couldn't believe that one woman's choice had impacted so many lives.

Cassie leaned over and picked up some of the scattered bits and pieces of paper littering the grave. "Secrets and lies," she murmured, rising to her feet. "My whole life was made up of secrets and lies."

Looking around, I caught snippets of my mother's poetry. I recognized familiar lines, seeing them with a new understanding. I could feel her guilt exposed on the page, the raw pain and emotion in every line. No wonder women still made the pilgrimage to her grave after all these years. She spoke to them. She spoke *for* them. Her voice was their own, crying out in pain and suffering. She turned their anguish into words and shouted them to the world.

No matter how much she railed on paper, however, my mother couldn't silence the demons in her own mind. Those demons are what ultimately took her from us.

I stood and reached for Cassie's hand. "There are no more secrets now. We can let go." I felt so much love for my sister. I couldn't believe I'd almost thrown it all away. Never again would I take this precious life for granted.

We walked back to the car, our fingers linked together. An errant breeze sent a swirl of leaves skittering along the path, teasing the air with a hint of spring. For the first time I noticed the colors around us: a riot of wildflowers bloomed among grass so green it seemed to glow from within. Earthen vases filled with lush floral arrangements adorned many headstones. The gray shades of winter were replaced with the new birth of spring.

I saw the world with fresh eyes. How could I have been so blinded by despair? I'd carried those black crayons from my past into adulthood, seeing the world in shades of gray. Now that I'd left the shadows behind, the world was beautiful in a way I'd never appreciated before.

Cassie dropped me off at the house. I tried to convince her to stay for dinner, but she begged off, saying she had some research to do. I had a feeling she was going to try to find our brother. I could have told her I'd already found him, but that would have raised questions I had no way of answering.

I remembered the doctor I'd seen at the hospital. He hadn't responded when I'd called him Parker, but I knew he was my brother just the same. Except in this lifetime he'd been raised by someone other than my mother. He had no idea she'd gone to her grave thinking he was dead, or that he had two sisters determined to find him.

I wondered what his life had been like growing up. Had he wondered about his birth family? Would he welcome us with open arms? Maybe he was content with the life he had and couldn't make room for two sisters who were strangers to him.

I had to think that we were meant to find each other in this life as well as the last. From my experience, even though we moved in separate directions, the people who matter are meant to cross paths at some point. I believed that Parker was one of those people. Whether I engineered this meeting or it came farther down the road, it was meant to be. Perhaps the reason I'd been sent to this timeline was to reunite Parker with the family he'd never known.

With that thought in mind, I made my way through the empty house. Bob was still at work. He'd left right behind us this morning to show houses to some clients. I'd been strangely relieved to discover he was back in real estate. It meant I was getting closer to my own timeline, the one where I'd first met Bob at the House of Cry.

I brewed a cup of tea, then settled down with the book Maya had left on my mother's grave. I recognized some of the markings in the margins. I'd seen her making them when I sat across from her at the library. It didn't surprise me to realize that some physical objects could travel across the timelines as well. After all, hadn't I carried my mother's poem and the Dorothy figurine with me the first time I'd crossed over? The second time I'd brought the tree pin Parker had given me. Obviously anything I was wearing or carrying made the voyage with me. Otherwise I'd arrive naked in my new reality—and wouldn't that raise a few eyebrows? I opened the page to the drawing Maya had made of a tree. Was it a coincidence that it mirrored the pin Parker had given me? Obviously Maya wanted me to see the connection. The tree was a symbolic representation of the ideas that had started to coalesce in my mind.

Choices. What if every choice one made split reality into two separate paths, like the branches of a tree? What if all those choices coexisted on some level? That would explain these diverse realities.

Most of the little day-to-day choices made no difference to the quality of life. Green beans or asparagus? Comedy or drama? Tiny branches that weave in and intersect but do nothing to change the overall structure.

But the big decisions, the ones that split a life into two diverse directions, those are the ones that change everything. That's where one becomes the *me-who-did* and the *me-who-did-not*. It was all about choices—not necessarily making the right choices, which is something we've been taught to believe, but making the most of all possible choices.

I touched the juncture where the trunk split into two separate limbs. If this represented my father's ultimatum, then on one side my mother chose Parker. Although my father tried to live with it, he eventually left, and Cassie was never born. On the other side, my mother chose her husband over her child and never forgave herself, ultimately taking her own life.

While I'd briefly had a taste of the world where my mother had made a choice she could live with, I also understood that within that world there were as many alternate possibilities as there were branches on a tree. But those were worlds I had no desire to return to. The world I wanted was on this branch, where my mother had made a different choice. This branch was where Cassie existed. It wasn't perfect, but it was the reality I knew best and the one I could take steps to improve day by day.

I ran my finger along the limb that represented the timeline I was currently on until I reached the next major fork. I already knew that Diane's wedding was an important turning point. After choosing to go to Diane's wedding, I'd met and ultimately married Bob, which led me to where I was right now. I needed to get back to the branch where I'd stayed home with Cassie that day. That would bring me closer to the path I'd slipped off when I'd fallen into the secret room. As much as I would have loved to stay here with a loving husband, a charming home, and a future bright with possibility, this wasn't my world.

If I followed my own path back to the beginning, would I find a choice I'd regret? An opportunity passed? Would I give up those years of raising my sister? No. Not for either of us, because looking back I had learned more than I was able to teach.

The only regret I had was letting someone else's decisions color the rest of my life. I couldn't control my mother's choices, only my reaction to their effect on my own life. Whatever I did from then on was my path, my branch.

And yet, all these alternate lives belonged to me. Looking back, I could see each path going back to the beginning. I understood on a certain level that my consciousness split and lived each and every alternate life fully. But the memory for each parallel universe was linear, moving back from each limb to the beginning, not able to see all the other branches in between.

I didn't need Maya to tell me I was right. Tracing the branches of the tree, it made perfect sense to me. If every possibility existed, then there was no right or wrong. In the end we'd be able to look back and see a life lived fully, see every single outcome and each lesson learned. Even our failures were important. At the end, there's a life path where every wrong decision was made, a path where every right decision was made, and every variation in between.

My tea had grown cold. I got up and made a fresh cup. The worst part was that I had no one to talk to about my theory. There was no one to convince me, even half-heartedly, that I wasn't crazy. But I didn't feel crazy. If anything, I felt saner than I'd ever felt. I felt sane and optimistic and incredibly free of guilt. I wasn't a failure. I was simply living one of an infinite number of realities. Maybe not the best one, but that didn't have to stop me from making it the best it could be.

Present lifeline included. I had a feeling that since I'd learned the lesson of this life, my time here would soon be coming to an end. But even if I had to go, could I leave without telling Cassie what I knew about our brother? I ripped a page from the book and scribbled his name in the margin—*Daniel Cody, M.D.* I folded the paper and tucked it into an envelope, wrote Cassie's name on the outside, then tucked it between the pages of my journal. I wasn't ready to reveal it yet, but if something happened to me Cassie would find his name here. I knew that when the time was right she'd find Parker and begin to heal some of our old family wounds, whether I was here to experience it or not.

Telling Cassie the truth right now could be a risk. She already felt vulnerable, as if everyone in her life had lied to her. Would she feel even more betrayed to find out I knew our brother's name? There was no way I could tell her I recognized him from another lifetime—not without a lengthy explanation at least. But I couldn't take a chance on her not being able to find him if I wasn't here to lead her in the right direction. I knew Cassie, and I knew she wouldn't rest until she'd found Parker and claimed him as family. With just one bold stroke I could save her years of fruitless searching.

It was a risk. The question was, should I take it?

I wished there was someone I could talk to about my decisions. I felt so alone. When I thought about sharing my burden, the first person I thought of was my friend Diane. She'd humored me once before. Would she do it again? After all, we had a lifetime of friendship to fall back on . . . at least in this timeline.

I picked up the phone before I could change my mind.

On the other end the phone rang three, four, five times. My heart sank when her voice mail picked up and I heard Diane's cheery voice: "Leave a message, I'll get back to you as soon as possible."

"Hi, Diane. It's Jenna. I, um, I just wanted to say thank you. We had a great time at dinner."

While I didn't want to do this on a recorded message, I felt that my time here was running out and there was so much more I needed to say. "I just want to tell you that I love you and how much I value our friendship. I promise I'll never do anything to let you down."

That wasn't enough, but it was a beginning. The real apology lay ahead of me, one I'd have to make to a friend I'd hurt deeply when I found my way back home. I only hoped Diane would be willing to accept it and welcome me back into her life.

———————

When Bob came home, I had a casserole bubbling away in the oven, along with a tray of homemade biscuits and a crisp green salad. The table was set with our best china, which sparkled in the glow of flickering candlelight.

"Special occasion?" he asked.

"I've decided that every day deserves to be a special occasion."

He tipped his head and smiled. "That's the Jenna I know and love."

I couldn't help myself. I had to ask, "What is it you love about me?"

He chuckled, then stopped and stared at me for a long moment. "You're serious, aren't you?"

I nodded. I had to know what someone could love about me, since I'd never been able to love myself.

He took my hand and led me to the couch, then sat beside me, one arm draped around my shoulder. The warmth of his body was inviting. I wanted to melt into his arms.

"First of all," he said, "what's not to love? You're everything I could ever want in a wife, lover, and best friend. You're smart and sweet, charming and generous. You put everyone else's needs before your own, sometimes to your own detriment. But I can't complain. That's the nurturer in you."

I dropped my gaze, knowing I didn't deserve the love in his eyes.

He reached out and ran a fingertip along my cheek. "Not to mention you're gorgeous with a banging body."

This time I had to laugh. "Banging, huh?"

He raised an eyebrow and let out a low, playful growl. "You know it, babe."

I picked up on his playfulness. "So you married me for my body?"

"No, I *noticed* you because of your body. I married you because I couldn't imagine my life without you."

I let out a slow, wistful sigh. I wanted to be that woman who inspired love and adoration. I wanted to be the kind of woman a man couldn't imagine living without.

His voice grew serious. "You helped me through some of the worst times of my life. You were my strength when Brett died."

"Brett?"

He shook his head. "I'm sorry. I forgot that you don't remember. Brett was my brother. He and his wife were killed in a plane crash."

I squeezed his hand in understanding. I knew how it felt to lose someone.

"You were my strength. You took care of everyone, including their daughter. You took her under your wing and helped her deal with her grief. I don't know how any of us would have coped without you."

I wanted to ask more about this side of the family that I had no memory of, but I could see that the wound was still fresh, and the last thing I wanted to do was dredge up more pain.

"So," he said, "is it any wonder I love you?"

Something inside me shifted as I began to see myself through his eyes. Was I that person? Did I deserve to be loved?

He leaned over to press a kiss to my cheek, but I surprised us both by turning to meet his lips with mine. I wrapped my arms around his neck and savored the sweetness, pressing my body against his with a languid stretch. His heartbeat quickened against mine. When my lips parted to explore the contours of his mouth, he let out a soft moan. "I've missed you," he whispered.

"I'm here now."

He tore his lips from mine and searched my eyes. "Are you? Are you really here now?"

I looked away. I couldn't lie to him. "I'm trying to be," I said. He had no idea how much I wanted to merge the life I remembered with the life he was ready to give me.

"What if we'd never met?" I asked him.

"We were meant to be together," he said with a genuine smile. "Somehow we'd have found each other."

Yes, one way or another. It gave me hope for all those other lives where we had yet to meet. Maybe destiny would find a way for us to cross paths, even if it was in some dim and distant future.

"Come on," I said. "Dinner is ready." I stood up, missing his closeness already. Bob set the table, giving me time to collect my thoughts while I put the finishing touches on the salad. There was something so natural about the way we worked together, like a perfectly choreographed team. I suspected we'd played these roles a hundred times or more, but for me it was brand new. So was the undercurrent of seduction in the seemingly casual movements—a touch, a glance, the brush of his hip against mine. I hoped the flush rising to my cheeks would be blamed on the heat of the oven. But I knew better.

I watched Bob over dinner. How easy it would be to settle into the comfortable role of loving wife. It was so tempting to stay here where I was loved, to ease back into the safety of his arms. But that would mean accepting a love I hadn't earned. It would be like living a lie. A sweet lie, but a lie all the same.

I pushed my food around the plate. I'd lost interest in eating. All I could think about was how it felt to kiss Bob. I glanced up and caught him staring at me. I felt warmth rise to my cheeks. Was he thinking what I was thinking?

I reached for a biscuit and took my time spreading butter from one edge to the other. I cleared my throat and tested my voice. "So, how long have we lived here in the House of . . . this house?"

"Only a few years," he replied. "We fell in love with the place the moment we saw it. Funny thing, it had been sitting vacant for a few months but had only gone on the market the week we started looking for a house."

"Curious."

"Yeah, almost like we were meant to be here."

That didn't surprise me. I was starting to see that no matter how much the different life paths diverged, some things remained constant, circling back and around as if they were meant to be. Maybe certain people, places, or events were touchstones that intersected each reality. Maybe Maya was one of those touchstones.

Bob cleared his throat. "What are you thinking about?"

"Oh, not much," I replied. "Life, death, and eternity."

He chuckled. "Nothing too deep, huh?"

I had a sudden thought. "Bob, do you know a woman named Maya? An older woman, about my height, maybe sixty years old?"

"Maya?" He tipped his head thoughtfully. "Like the poet?"

The poet? Of course, Maya Angelou. Why hadn't I made the connection? "Yeah, like the poet," I said. Was it a coincidence that I'd replaced one mother figure with another who just happened to share a famous poet's name? Even more reason to believe Maya was simply a figment of my imagination. A psychologist would have a field day with this.

Bob thought about my question for a few moments. "No, can't say I know anyone by that name. Why?"

"I don't know. I just heard it somewhere, I guess."

He stood up and began clearing plates from the table. "Maybe that's a sign you're getting your memory back."

I helped clear the table. "I think you're right." We worked together side by side at the sink, washing and drying in tandem. It felt natural, like a nightly routine.

"You're good at this," I said. "You should do it for a living." It was meant as a joke, but then I remembered the conversation I'd had with Bob in my last reality. "Have you ever thought of opening a bed-and-breakfast?"

He tipped his head and gave me an odd smile. "Funny you should say that. It's a dream I've always had, but . . ." He looked away.

"But what?"

"But it would be risky. There's no telling how long it would take to get off the ground. We probably wouldn't have a regular income for a while." He dried the last dish, then draped the dish towel over the sink. "It would be one thing if I only had myself to worry about, but I have a wife to consider, and possibly a family on the way."

A family. Now there was something to think about.

"Speaking of family," I said. "I found out some things about my mother today."

"Oh?"

I took a deep breath and told Bob everything I'd learned from my father, letting the words tumble out in one long, rambling sentence. "All these years we never knew."

"That's incredible," Bob said, rubbing my shoulders. "Do you want to find him? I can hire a private detective. Or maybe we should start by searching on the Internet. I bet there are websites that deal with reuniting adoptive siblings."

God, I wanted to hug him. His first instinct was to figure out how he could help me, and he was ready to jump right into the fray. How had I gotten so lucky?

I wrapped my arms around his waist and rested my head on his shoulder. "Thank you."

He held me close. I took a deep breath, inhaling his scent. It triggered a flurry of sensations, from my chest all the way to my core. I pressed my body against his, and the sensations swelled and deepened. His response was immediate, letting me know just how much he missed his wife.

I knew I shouldn't, but it didn't matter. My body's needs outweighed my brain's discretion. I reached up and ran my fingers through his hair. It curled along the base of his neck, as if he'd gone a little too long between haircuts. I slid my fingers into the thick, dark waves and tugged gently. He moaned in response.

On some deep, instinctive level I knew all the places to touch and kiss and fondle to bring out the beast inside him. He responded with an ardor that had been held in check for too long, sweeping me up in a passionate embrace and clutching me tight against him. I knew his body as well as my own, from the wide expanse of chest to the curve of his abdomen and the tight, hard swell of his groin. I didn't know how I knew, but I did, and that knowledge came with a sense of possessiveness. This man was mine.

The knowledge that my time here could end at any moment only fueled my desire. "I want you," I said, a husky edge to my voice. "I want you now."

I didn't have to ask twice.

———————

I lay awake long after Bob had fallen asleep. My body felt limp and languid, like warm taffy. I stretched and let out a slow, satisfied sigh. If Bob hadn't been perfect for me in every other way, I'd marry him all over again just for the sex alone.

I rolled over and braced myself on one elbow, studying his face. His mouth was slightly open, his breath soft and warm. He looked so vulnerable in sleep. "I'll find you again," I whispered. "I promise to find you, no matter how long it takes or how many lifetimes I have to search for you."

He mumbled in his sleep, then turned and settled into his pillow. I leaned over and brushed my lips along his temple, then climbed out of bed. I stood naked in the dusky darkness and ran my hand down my belly. We hadn't used protection tonight. I wondered if we'd made a baby. Surely in one of my lifetimes there would be children to raise, a family to love.

Up until this moment I hadn't realized how much I wanted a family. Suddenly it was all I could think about. A little boy with Bob's strong jaw and dark hair, a girl I could dress in pink and have tea parties with.

I slipped on a robe and headed for the bathroom, padding quietly in the dark so as not to wake Bob. I wondered if he, too, wanted a family. I'd ask him in the morning. There were so many things I wanted to know about him. I wanted to learn more about his family, the niece he tried to be a father figure to. Where was she now? What about his parents? Were they still alive?

I wanted to make love to him over and over again—day and night, night and day. I wanted to ravish him in the living room, seduce him in the shower, and savor every inch of him in the kitchen.

———————

Maybe it was because I wanted it so much that everything else began to fade into the background. As weeks drifted by, I slipped into the routine of daily life easily, comfortably. I thrived on married life as if I were born to be half of a couple. Thoughts of finding Parker fell by the wayside. Eventually all thoughts of my prior lives became misty and dreamlike. Days would go by when

I didn't think of my past at all. Why would I when the present was everything I could ever have imagined?

I sat at the bedroom window. A shadow seemed to form just out of my vision. I tried to focus, but it was gone. Bob caught me staring out the window. "Hey, sleepyhead. Time to get dressed. People will be arriving in a few hours."

I turned and smiled. Our anniversary.

He crossed the room and wrapped his arms around me. "Can you believe we've been married five years?" I nuzzled my face against his neck, inhaling the scent of him. Starch on his collar, the tang of his aftershave, so familiar, so dear. My heart still fluttered when I looked at his face. I remembered the first time I saw him standing in the doorway of . . . what? That wasn't right. I shook my head. We had met at Diane's wedding six years ago, the night of Cassie's accident. How could I have forgotten?

And yet another image overlapped that one: Cassie unscarred and smiling, introducing me to Bob at the House of . . . House of . . . *something*. I shook the false memory away. All that mattered was that I was here now, in the arms of the man I loved and about to celebrate our anniversary with friends and family.

I took my time, steaming under a long, luxurious shower. I took extra care with my hair and picked out one of Bob's favorite outfits to wear. When I came into the kitchen, I noticed a vase holding five pink carnations—one for each year we were married.

When Cassie came to the door carrying a large sheet cake, the sight of her scars caught me by surprise.

"Why do you always do that?" she asked, standing in the doorway with the cake.

"Do what?"

"Act like it's the first time you've seen my face like this."

Why? Guilt maybe. But there was more to it than that. Those scars didn't belong there. Each time I saw them I was overcome by a sense of wrongness. I started to explain but was distracted by a shadow lurking in the distance. "What was that?"

Cassie turned to where I was pointing. "Where? I don't see anything."

Too late. The shadow had melted into the distance. But something told me it wouldn't be the last time I'd see it. And whatever it was couldn't be good.

Cassie brushed by me and placed the cake on the countertop. She gave Bob a kiss on the cheek. "How have you put up with her all these years?"

He chuckled, but I suspected Cassie was only half joking. Some part of her must still blame me for her disfigurement. It was something I couldn't take back, no matter how many times I apologized.

There wasn't time, however, because Diane and Dean were at the door. Diane carried a bottle of wine. "It's all yours," she said. "I can't drink while I'm breastfeeding."

Dean trailed behind, carrying the baby in an infant seat. Bob reached for the baby, but Dean pushed him away. "Don't wake her up," he shushed. "She may look like an angel, but she screams like a demon. Enjoy the silence while you can."

"I'll get to hold her eventually, though, won't I?"

Dean placed the carrier gently on the table. "Nope. She's mine. Go get one of your own." He glanced knowingly at me, and I felt the color rise to my cheeks.

Bob laughed. "This from the guy who painted 'No Girls Allowed' all over the tree house.

"Yeah, well, that's when we didn't like girls." He gazed lovingly at the rosy-cheeked angel sleeping soundly in the infant carrier. "My job now is to keep her away from guys like us in the future."

The rest of the day went smoothly. We ate cake and reminisced and took turns playing with the baby. I couldn't wait to have one of my own, but until then I'd enjoy playing godmother to Diane's child.

When everyone left, Bob began emptying the dishwasher while I picked up. Again I noticed a shadow standing in the yard. Only this time it took form, and I saw a face. A name floated into my memory.

Maya.

"Bob, I'm going for a walk. I'll be right back."

"Sure, hon." He turned and gave me a concerned look. "Are you okay?"

"Yes, I just need a little fresh air." But that was a lie. I wasn't all right, and I suspected once I faced the specter outside nothing would ever be all right again.

I caught up with Maya just beyond the garden. Her face was soft with sympathy, and she felt as light as smoke. "I know you, don't I?"

"Of course you do, child."

"But . . . I've forgotten."

"The longer you stay, the more you'll forget. Soon I'll be gone completely, along with any memories that don't belong to this branch of your life."

I tried to pretend I didn't understand, but it was all coming back to me. The longer I stared into Maya's eyes, the more I remembered.

I could have everything I wanted here: a devoted husband, a beautiful home, and even the promise of children. But at what cost? Could I choose my own happiness over the promise I'd made my sister?

"You're free to stay," Maya said, as if reading my mind. "But the longer you stay here, the more you'll forget. It's only natural. No one can hold the knowledge of each parallel life for long. It's natural to choose one to hold your consciousness. That's how people exist."

The hand she placed on my shoulder was lighter than a feather. "It's your choice, Jenna."

I gazed back wistfully at the house. This was where I wanted to be, but it wasn't where I *needed* to be.

"I can't imagine my life without him," I said, turning back. But Maya was gone. All that was left was the knowledge that I was about to give up everything I had with only the slimmest hope that I'd be able to find it again.

One more night, I pleaded silently. *One more night to spend with the man I love.*

I went back inside and stepped into my husband's embrace. "Happy anniversary," I whispered.

"Mmmm . . . happy anniversary, my love."

He leaned in for a kiss that was long and hard and full of promise. I arched against him, feeling the heat of his arousal pressed against my body. "We can clean up tomorrow," he said. "I have other plans for tonight."

I gave him my best come-hither smile. "Give me five minutes to get ready."

"Three," he said with a wolfish grin. "I can't wait any longer than that."

I turned and walked away, exaggerating the swing to my hips. I opened the bathroom door and stepped inside, but the room was all wrong. Before I could pinpoint the differences, the familiar vertigo hit me, and the room began to spin.

"No!" I cried, trying to step back. But it was too late. The secret room already had a hold on me. The room that shouldn't be there pulled me inside. I heard a soft rustling, like the whisper of lost souls. I felt they held the wisdom of the universe and the answers to questions I couldn't voice.

I couldn't move forward and couldn't retreat. The room held me suspended, as if waiting for permission to drag me forward into the unknown, away from this life I hadn't known I wanted and a man who couldn't imagine his own life without me. "No, not yet. Please . . ." But the words were powerless. Even as I cried out, I knew that I couldn't stay. I had to find my way back to the world where I belonged. With that thought alone, I surrendered and gave myself up to the inevitable.

The room dissolved around me, as if the very walls were made of tears.

15

I fought the rise to consciousness, drifting in and out, blissfully unaware of my surroundings. I dreamed of many paths, many lives. Familiar faces wove in and out of my dreams, turning strangers to friends and friends to strangers. I dreamed of joy and sorrow, births and deaths, of loves lost and lovers found over and over and over again.

I was afraid to open my eyes. As long as I kept them closed, I could pretend that Bob was in the bed beside me, that everything else was just a dream. I could feel the wedding ring on my finger. Surely that was all the proof I needed that I was still Mrs. Robert Hartwood, wasn't it?

As hard as I tried, a part of me knew that I was fooling myself. Bob was gone, everything was gone. The ring, like the poem and pin, had simply followed me to a new reality. For a moment I was insanely jealous of the version of myself that this ring actually belonged to. I thought of the engraving inside—*Everwhen*. Which everwhen had I found myself in this time?

"Open your eyes, Jenna. I know you're awake."

"No," I whimpered.

"Jenna." It was Maya's voice, coaxing me gently into this reality, like a midwife ushering a new life into the world.

"I don't want to, Maya. I want to go back."

She took my hand, her fingers warm and comforting around mine. "I'm sorry. You can't go back, child."

I let out a long, mournful sigh, then opened my eyes. My first thought was that I was back in the hospital. The room around me had that same sterile atmosphere, with walls painted an institutional shade of gray. I heard the rise and fall of voices outside the door. Many voices. "Where am I?"

"You're in a safe place," Maya said. "A place where you can't hurt yourself."

"Hurt myself. Why would I . . . ?" That's when I noticed the bandages wrapped with care around my wrists. I didn't have to ask what was hidden beneath the bandages. "My birthday, right?"

Maya nodded. She seemed distant, as if I'd let her down. And I had, hadn't I? I knew what was hidden beneath the stark white bandages. It was the truth I'd been avoiding all along.

Death.

I thought back to my birthday. The memory was vivid. I'd walked all alone to the cemetery and stood over my mother's grave. I'd held the razor against my wrist, visualizing how it would feel to push the cool metal deep into the skin. I could almost smell the copper tang of blood, feel the pain slicing my skin, and imagine the serene peace of letting go and floating into the great nowhere.

But I hadn't done it. At the last second I'd stopped myself, remembering my promise to Cassie. I'd flung away the unused razor and faced the prospect of another lonely birthday. It wasn't the first time I'd stared death in the face only to hear the ghostly echo of laughter mocking me. I'd escaped this time, but death always wins in the end.

Cassie had found me there at the cemetery and taken me to see the House of Cry. I remember the way she'd watched me carefully, as if sensing how close I'd come to the edge. It all seemed so long ago. I didn't even feel like the same person anymore.

"I didn't do it," I said. But that didn't matter, did it? The fact that I'd chosen not to kill myself only meant that reality had split in two that day and the opposite choice existed in another timeline. This timeline.

With brilliant clarity I realized that there were no right choices and no wrong choices. All of our choices are played out somewhere, somehow. Here I was on the other side of that choice, my wrists scarred, my relationships destroyed. "I'm sorry."

"You've let a lot of people down," Maya said sadly. "Including yourself."

I rubbed the bandages, feeling the still raw wounds beneath the gauze. "Is this a hospital then?"

"It's a recovery center. Your sister had you admitted for your own safety."

A recovery center? Was that a fancy name for a psychiatric ward? I almost felt relieved. Hadn't I always worried that this was exactly where I'd end up one day? My worst fear had come true. And only now, for the first time in my life, was I one hundred percent sure that I didn't want to die.

I was almost afraid to ask the next question: "Did Cassie find me that morning?"

Maya nodded. "When you didn't answer the phone, she came looking for you. She found you lying on the ground, your life-blood seeping into the dirt of your mother's grave." Maya made a disapproving sound. "It broke her heart."

My chest tightened, as if my own heart were breaking. How could I have done that to Cassie? I was no better than our mother. I had to make it up to her somehow.

I tried to get out of bed, but Maya stopped me. "You can't leave," she said. "Not until someone signs your release."

"But I'm fine." I held up my arms. "It wasn't me who did this."

"Of course it was," Maya chided. "And now you have to learn to deal with the consequences."

She was right. I hadn't slashed my wrists, but the person who had needed to be here in this safe place. "Okay."

I could do this. After all, I was a seasoned traveler by now. I knew the ropes, which pitfalls to avoid. I'd find my way out of this reality and back to where I belonged. There had to be a way for me to get back to my own world without leaving my alter ego vulnerable.

"Maya," I said. "I figured it out. You know, about how the choices we make split into separate realities."

She patted my hand. "I knew you would."

"But one thing puzzles me," I said. "If we live all these different possible life lines, then which one counts?"

"They all do. Every outcome exists simultaneously. You need each branch to form a whole life."

"So it's not just about making the right choice every step of the way, is it? It's what we learn from the wrong ones, too."

She gave me a smile of approval, like a teacher rewarding a gifted student. "There is no right or wrong, no good or bad. There are only endless possibilities."

I frowned. "Then what's the point?"

She ran a fingertip over my furrowed brow. "Oh, child. The point is to experience every facet of life to its fullest. It *all* matters. Every choice, every thought, every dream."

"Even the pain and suffering?"

"Yes, even the pain and suffering. And the love and joy and moments of divine inspiration. Each separate branch is necessary to accumulate the knowledge and skills needed to move on."

I settled into the bed, feeling disjointed. "I'm sleepy."

"That's the medication they gave you. Rest now, child."

I grew drowsier but had one last question to ask Maya before she disappeared again. "Why doesn't everyone get to see their lives this way?"

Maya tilted her head and gave me an enigmatic smile. "What makes you think they don't?"

———————

The next morning Maya was gone. It didn't surprise me. I'd grown used to her disappearances.

A bright-eyed young woman entered the room carrying med-
ications in a small paper cup in one hand and a plastic glass of
water in the other. She reminded me of Cassie, sending a wave
of longing through me. I needed to talk to my sister. I had to tell
her how sorry I was and promise I'd never do anything so foolish
again. But would she believe my promises?

"Is there a phone I can use?" I asked the woman. She wore light-
blue hospital scrubs, but I wasn't sure if she was a doctor, nurse, or
orderly. "There's a public phone at the end of the hall and a sign-up
sheet at the front desk." She handed me the water and pills.

"Do I have to take these?" I couldn't tell her that I had no
need for antidepressants or antipsychotics or whatever these
pills might be.

"Doctor's orders," she said. "You're scheduled for a consultation at ten o'clock," she informed me. "If he doesn't think you need
the medication anymore, he can update your chart, okay?"

I didn't want to upset her, but I didn't want to take the pills
either. I'd need a clear head to convince everyone I was fine now. I
put the pills in my mouth and held them under my tongue while
swallowing a sip of water. I waited a reasonable amount of time,
then quietly coughed the pills into my palm and slipped them
between the sheets without any guilt. I was no danger to myself,
so the medication was unnecessary.

Once I was alone again, I explored the room. It was a private
room, more spacious than the hospital room I'd been in before. I
found my clothes hanging neatly in a small closet. I cleaned myself
up in the bathroom and did my best to make myself presentable.
I knew that appearances were half the battle, and I wanted to look
as sane as I felt.

I made my way to the front desk first, pleased to discover there
was a nine o'clock slot open on the telephone sign-up sheet. I wrote
my name down, then walked around to get my bearings. There
were no bars on the windows or doors. I could see well-manicured

grounds outside with winding walking paths. Visitors came and went, signing in at the desk. There was a community room with a television and game tables set up. This was obviously a high-end recovery center and had to be costing my sister more than she could afford. Even more reason for me to talk my way out of here.

When it came time to make my call, I was relieved to see a telephone book nearby. Just to be safe, I double-checked Cassie's number. It was the same one I remembered, which was a good sign that I was getting closer to the timeline from which I'd started.

I held my breath, waiting through one ring. Two. Three. When Cassie finally answered, I released the breath I'd been holding and let out a long, grateful sigh. "It's me," I said.

"Jenna?" Cassie sounded guarded, but it was good to hear her voice.

"I'm sorry," I said, although I was sure I'd probably said it a thousand times already.

"How are you feeling?" she asked, ignoring my apology.

"Better." That, at least, was the truth. "You don't have to worry anymore. I promise." As soon as the words left my mouth, I knew it was the wrong thing to say.

"Don't make promises you can't keep," she said. I could hear the hurt and betrayal in her voice, and it broke my heart. "How could you do this, Jenna?" Cassie asked. "You of all people. You know what suicide does to the people left behind."

I wanted to shout to her that yes, I knew, and that's what ultimately had saved me. I'd remembered my promise never to leave Cassie all alonely and had kept that promise. I'd made the right choice to save my own life. This one was the mistake. "I'm sorry." That was all I could manage to say.

"I'll come by to see you tomorrow, okay?"

I knew that despite everything she still loved me. It was a start. "Okay. But I just have to ask one thing. I know this is going to sound crazy, but do you remember the day Diane got married?"

"Huh? Yeah, of course I remember. You stayed home with me because I was sick that day. Boy, was Diane pissed." I could hear the puzzlement in her voice. "Why?"

"Nothing," I said. A sigh of relief escaped my lips. This was another sign that I was closer to my real world. But I wasn't there yet. I still had to get back to the secret room. One more jump should bring me home. But a shadow crossed over my heart. That meant I hadn't yet met Bob. "I love you, Cassie."

It hurt to hear the hesitation in her voice. Finally she answered, "I love you too, Sis. Are you sure you're okay?"

"Yes. I have a consultation with the doctor in about an hour. I'm sure he'll have good news for both of us."

At least I hoped so. I had a good feeling that once I resolved whatever problems I had to conquer in this timeline, my next shift would take me back where I belonged. And when I did, I'd arrive with a changed attitude and a renewed sense of purpose. I just had to get there.

I sat in the waiting area trying to convince myself that I would be able to talk my way out of here. I wasn't crazy. Depressed, maybe. But even that seemed to belong to a long-ago life. It usually started in the months leading up to my birthday, the anniversary of my mother's death. Depression would creep in slyly. One day I'd realize that I hadn't shaved my legs in a few weeks. The dishes would start stacking up in the sink. Bills piled up, unopened and unpaid. I simply stopped caring. Every little thing took too much effort. Being around people was exhausting, and I couldn't wait to be alone again to drop the charade.

But that was then, not now. And I certainly wasn't crazy. Did anyone even use the word "crazy" anymore? There were a million different labels, letters strung together like pearls on a string to describe the many forms of mental illness. Not me, though. I was fine. I just had to convince everyone else. Once I was free, I could find my way back to the House of Cry and the secret room that would lead me home.

"Dr. Cody will see you now."

I should have recognized the name right away, but it didn't click. Not until I opened the door and saw a familiar face. "Parker?"

He looked up. "I beg your pardon?"

I shook my head. I'd been down this route before. "Nothing," I said, taking a seat across the desk. The name plate said *Daniel Cody, M.D.* I should have been surprised, but I wasn't. Somehow in all these divergent paths there remains a pattern. There are sacred places, people who are important in all of your journeys, and lessons learned despite yourself. Everything circles back—the right and wrong, the real and false. It all circles back.

I studied the man behind the desk. His hair was the same color as mine, but he had Cassie's eyes. I could see my mother in his face as well. Why hadn't I noticed before? I knew the answer. I hadn't really looked at him. As usual I'd been too caught up in my own private drama to be aware of anything or anyone else.

He opened a folder on his desk. "So, how are you feeling today, Jenna?"

"Good," I said. "Really good. Better than ever."

He looked up and held my gaze. Maybe I had come off as a little too manic in my effort to sound sane.

"You know you can tell me anything, right?"

I could, couldn't I? It was his job to listen to me, no matter how delusional I sounded. That gave me an idea. What was the harm? I was already locked up.

I leaned forward. "This is going to sound really off the wall, but there is something I'd like to talk to you about."

He nodded, giving me permission to continue. "Go ahead."

"Imagine if every time you made a choice it changed reality. If you go left, another version of you goes right. Imagine that all these different realities existed simultaneously."

"The Many-Worlds Theory."

This time I was the one taken by surprise. "There's a theory? A scientific theory?" And here I was so proud of myself for figuring it out.

"Well, quantum physics. That's not exactly the same thing. Isn't that what you're referring to?"

"Um, yes. Of course." Maybe this wasn't going to be as hard as I thought. At least I didn't have to explain what I was talking about. I just had to convince him that it was true. "So imagine that every choice you make splits off into one of these many worlds. Then you'd be living different versions of your life simultaneously."

"That's one way of looking at it."

"So, hypothetically speaking, what if you were able to cross over into one of these parallel lives and see people you thought were dead, or discover relatives you didn't know you had?"

His face gave nothing away, but I recognized the look in his eyes. I'd seen that same look in Parker's eyes when I'd messed up the job interview he'd arranged for me.

"Oh, fuck it," I said. If Parker/Dan was my psychiatrist, then he was obligated to listen to me whether he wanted to or not. I might as well get it all out. "Here's the thing. About a week ago, I woke up in an alternate reality where my dead mother was alive, and I had a brother I'd never met before."

His eyes widened, but that was the only emotion he allowed to slip out. He was as stoic as his parallel counterpart.

"You were that brother," I said, leaning forward. "In this alternate reality, we'd grown up together even though I didn't recognize you then. I found out later that my mother had given you up for adoption in my own timeline. You *were* adopted, weren't you?"

He didn't miss a beat. "This is about you, not me."

I knew I'd struck a nerve, however. "Look at me. Can't you see the family resemblance?"

I tried a different tactic. "How many patients have you interviewed? Hundreds? Thousands? I'm sure you can tell the difference between a patient who's delusional and one who is telling the truth, no matter how outrageous it sounds."

He avoided my gaze. "I've also spoken to patients who invented elaborate fantasies to justify their behavior."

"Well, that's not the case here. I'm not delusional. I'm telling you the truth."

"The truth is you're here because you attempted suicide."

I shook my head. "Suicide is the last thing on my mind. You know that my mother committed suicide, don't you?"

I answered my own question. "Of course you do. It's right there in my file." I gave a little snort. "In my own world I always worried that I'd end up just like my mother. Turned out to be a self-fulfilling prophecy, huh?"

He made no move to agree or disagree.

"But only in this world," I continued. "In my real world I chose not to commit suicide. I kept my promise to my sister that I'd never leave her, never do what our mother did. That's the world I'm trying to get back to."

He leaned back in his chair and tapped his chin with the eraser end of his pencil. "So what you're saying is that you want to go back to a time before you attempted suicide."

"Yes. No." I saw exactly where he was going. "What I mean is, that timeline already exists."

"A timeline where your mother is still alive?"

"Yes. And that's not some form of wish fulfillment." I realized I was getting nowhere and decided to change the subject. "You know who my mother is, right?"

"Marjorie Parker Hall."

"Yes. Have you read any of her poetry?"

"Of course."

"How did it make you feel? Did it resonate with you in any way?"

He shook his head. "I can't say that it did."

"You should read them again," I said. "I think you'll feel differently now, knowing she's *your* mother, too."

He gave his head a single shake of denial. I knew I'd gone too far for one day. Maybe if I gave it some time to sink in, he'd be open to hearing more of my outrageous theories. Maybe during our next consultation I'd tell him about all the worlds I'd seen and how many ways our lives intertwined. I'd tell him about Cassie and Bob and . . . no, not Maya. There was a limit to how much I could expect anyone to suspend their disbelief. It was hard enough getting him to believe that I'd experienced several parallel realities without throwing in a guardian angel or spirit guide or whatever Maya might be.

"I'm not asking you to take everything I say on faith. I'm just asking you to listen, to think about what I've said. You might want to do a little research on your own about your roots. I think you'll be surprised."

There, I'd made my case. There was nothing more I could do. I was getting ready to leave when he spoke up. "You called me Parker."

"Parker was my mother's maiden name. I guess it was her way of announcing to the world that you belonged to her. You were a Parker."

He made a snorting sound, but the fact that he'd even asked proved to me he was willing to think about what I'd said.

———

I had the rest of the day to myself. I wanted to walk through the front door and keep on going. But what good would that do me? I didn't even know how far I was from the House of Cry, let alone how to get there on foot. I had no money, no credit cards, and no form of identification. But that wasn't the only thing. I had a feeling that I needed to be here. Whatever issues I had to resolve before moving on were right here within these walls.

To my surprise, I found there was plenty to do. There were planned activities, group therapy, arts and crafts, and a common recreation room with a television and table games. It was a little like camp, except I felt that I was under constant observation. I was afraid of saying the wrong thing, doing the wrong thing, choosing the wrong color bead to string onto a necklace that no one in their right mind would wear. But then, was anyone here in his or her right mind?

My fellow patients suffered from just about every diagnosis possible: manic depression, schizophrenia, alcohol and drug addiction, eating disorders, obsessive-compulsive disorders, and—like myself—attempted suicide.

I struck up a conversation with a young girl wearing all black, with silver rings piercing her eyebrows. Her skin was pale, with self-inflicted scars along her arms that formed a delicate filigree pattern. It seemed less like mutilation and more like art, combining self-harm with scarification.

She said her name was Lorelei but occasionally failed to answer to it. When I first saw her, she was reading *Eat, Pray, Love* with a combination of longing and disdain. She glanced up from her book and patted the seat beside her. "I was wondering when you were going to get here."

I sat down. Obviously this wasn't our first meeting, but I found myself wondering what we had in common—other than the fact that we both wore our scars on the outside.

"Meat loaf is on the menu tonight," she said. "I heard someone once found a tooth in the meat loaf." She leaned closer and whispered, "It was a human tooth."

To be honest, I'm not sure which would creep me out more— human or animal. "I think I'll skip the meat loaf."

"Good choice." She stood up. "Let's go for a walk."

I followed her to the front desk, where she put our names on a list. The man at the desk glanced at the sheet, then back at us. "Half an hour," he said. "Group therapy is at three o'clock."

Lorelei gave him a forced smile. "Oh, we'll be back in plenty of time. Don't want to miss group therapy, do we, Jenna?"

I followed her lead. "No, of course not," I said brightly.

"You get more points by smiling and being polite," she said, leading me outside. We walked leisurely, followed a well-defined path through the woods. "I learned that the hard way," she said.

I knew all about putting on a false face for the world. The old me would get up in the morning, do my hair and makeup, then carefully construct the face I wanted the world to see. It was important to hide my real face from the people around me. It was even more important to hide it from myself, even if this false face was only an illusion. But carrying on a charade can be exhausting. It was easier to avoid people altogether, to hide behind drawn curtains stripped of the mask of self-delusion.

But that was the old me. I'd changed, even more than I could have imagined. Only now did I see how deeply I had been trapped beneath the shroud of depression. I found it somewhat ironic that only now that I was no longer depressed did I find myself in a recovery center getting the help I needed years ago.

I looked around at the peaceful setting. "So, we're just allowed to walk wherever we want?"

"Sure, if wherever you want is through the woods on the property. I've heard of people trying to make a break for it, but the highway is about ten miles in either direction. We're pretty much in the middle of nowhere."

For some reason her answer gave me comfort. As long as escape was an impossibility, then I didn't have to waste time and energy figuring out how to make a break for it.

"I saw your name on the phone log this morning," Lorelei said. "Did you call your sister?"

"Yep. She's coming by tomorrow."

Lorelei snorted. "That's what she said yesterday."

I stumbled but caught myself before falling. Lorelei didn't seem to notice.

"You know, I think your sister is a little afraid to come out here."

"Why would you say that?"

"Because she's no different than we are. Cassie lost her mother, too. She didn't escape unscathed."

Ah, now it made sense. This was what Lorelei and I had in common. I should have realized, since my mother's death was what had defined me for so long. Wounded souls had a tendency to find each other. Maybe it was a way of proving we were not alone.

"What was it like for you?" she asked.

"You mean watching my mother's slow descent into madness?"

Lorelei nodded.

"It was like she was balanced on a high wire, way above my head, too far away to hear my cries. I'd watch each teetering stumble, my heart in my throat, holding my breath and mentally preparing my grief for the inevitable fall."

"I almost envy you," Lorelei said. "At least you had some warning. With me it was so sudden, so unexpected. One minute my life was perfect, and the next everything had changed."

I understood how she felt. "It's like your life is forever split into before and after, right?"

"Yeah," she said. Her voice held a hollow tone, devoid of life. "You go on, but all the time you're building up scar tissue." She traced a fingertip along the scars on her inner arm. "Sometimes you build up so much scar tissue that it's impossible to find the person hidden underneath."

She took a deep breath, then let it out slowly. "Sometimes I just get tired, you know? Tired of putting one foot in front of the other. Tired of making choices. Tired of waiting for the end."

I wanted to cry for the wounded child walking beside me, but I knew better than to shed a tear. If I started crying, I might never stop.

16

Meals were served cafeteria style, with men and women seated separately—males with males and females with females. No comingling was allowed.

I slid my tray along the metal rack. A woman wearing a hairnet and a scowl asked if I wanted meat loaf or a sandwich.

I pretended to consider the options. "What kind of sandwich?"

"Peanut butter and jelly."

Lorelei jabbed me from behind. "That'll do," I said.

The woman gave Lorelei a sharp glance.

Lorelei smiled and shrugged innocently. "Make that two."

We wound our way to a corner table. "You made that up about the meat loaf, didn't you?"

"I can't take credit for it. The legend has been passed down through the years to warn people away from eating the meat loaf. Believe me, it's for your own good."

"Yeah, but I'll probably never be able to eat meat loaf again now."

"You should consider becoming a vegetarian."

"You're not the first person to suggest that," I muttered.

Lorelei carefully cut the crusts from her sandwich with a plastic knife, then cut it corner to corner into four perfect triangles. She shook two packets of artificial sweetener and sprinkled them into her iced tea. "You could still have macaroni and cheese," she offered sagely. "Which I think is the perfect food. Other than pizza."

There was something comforting about her rambling. It made me think of evenings spent at the dinner table chatting with Cassie. Outwardly they were nothing alike, but appearances were deceiving. Both chattered to cover the silences. Silences could be dangerous. They left too much room for reflection.

Lorelei glanced at me. "What are you smiling about?"

"You remind me of Cassie when she was younger."

"She was a pain in the ass?"

I laughed. "No, she was sweet and funny and a bit of a chatterbox. Like you."

Lorelei blushed and lowered her gaze, acting as if she couldn't care less, but I could see through her tough exterior. I knew she was touched by the comparison.

"So," she said, "Cassie was more like a daughter than a sister, huh?"

"I guess you could say that, except we kind of grew up together. Sometimes Cassie resents it when I get all motherly with her, because I'm only five years older than she is."

Lorelei let out a slow sigh. "Yeah, a big sister's not the same as a real mother." She frowned, then glanced away. "But it's better than no mother at all."

My heart broke at the yearning in her voice. I reached across the table to tuck a stray hair behind her ear, and she closed her eyes, perhaps remembering the long-ago touch of her own mother's hand. I wished there were more I could do to help ease her pain.

When she spoke again, all the hardness had seeped away, leaving behind the wistful voice of a child. "I think you'd be a good mother," she said.

I thought of Bob and was overcome with an overwhelming feeling of loss for the children we'd never have together. "I think so, too," I said over the lump in my throat.

"I think I'd be a good mother, too," Lorelei said. "But if I had a daughter, I wouldn't read her fairy tales or let her believe in happy endings. There are no happy endings."

She punctuated the air with her sandwich. "If I had a daughter, I'd teach her to fight and slay her own dragons. I'd tell her to live her life exactly how she wants to. Live it for herself, and if Prince Charming comes along, he's welcome to share it with her. If not, she'll be fine without him."

"That's wonderful advice," I said. "For all of us, not just our daughters."

She nodded, chewing thoughtfully. "Yes, you're right. I can be my own daughter, can't I?"

"We can all be our own daughters, our own mothers, and our own sisters. We should take charge of our lives and fill in the empty emotional spaces. It shouldn't matter whether we were loved enough as long as we learn to love ourselves."

"I can do that," she said. "I can learn to love myself, can't I?"

I clasped her hand in mine. "Of course you can, Lorelei. You're extremely lovable."

And I meant that. In the real world we'd never have met. We had nothing in common. And yet we'd found so many points of interest and become friends here in this fishbowl. Maybe recovery was possible when people shared strengths rather than focusing on weaknesses. I made a mental note to find this sweet, wounded child once I got back to my own timeline. Maybe I could become the big sister she'd never had and help her fulfill her potential.

I'd spent too long being self-absorbed, unaware that everyone carries their own private pain. There was so much I could do if I only reached out. Who better to help heal another than someone who'd come out of the darkness and into the light? Hadn't Bob said that my desire to take care of other people was one of the qualities he loved most about me?

But what about the "me" I'd be leaving behind? I was only an observer here, a traveling ghost haunting an alternate version of myself. What would happen when I moved on? Who would help her out of the darkness? While I was busy trying to escape recovery, she'd still be in need of it, along with the therapy Parker could provide. Would he believe me and treat her with kindness and understanding? Would he be mindful of her memory gaps? It was up to me to make sure that when I moved on to the next reality she'd be taken care of.

Lorelei and I spent the rest of our dinner hour laughing and gossiping. I learned more about her life and shared some of my own with her. When she asked about the wedding ring I still wore, I pretended I'd bought it myself to avoid unwelcome attention from men.

"Why? Don't you like men?"

"Oh, I like men fine enough. It's just that for a long time I didn't think I was ready to make a commitment to someone else. Now, I think I like myself enough to be a good wife and mother."

"How do you get to that place?" she asked. "You know, the *liking yourself* place?"

Good question. One I probably couldn't have answered a few days ago. "I think part if it is realizing that no matter how far off track you get, it's never too late to turn your life around."

She glanced pointedly at my bandaged wrists.

"Almost never," I said.

I twirled the wedding band around my finger, feeling like a hypocrite. Bob didn't know me in this timeline, so I had no right to wear it. I reflected about what I'd said to Lorelei. I *was* ready for a committed relationship now. Then why was I hesitant to call Bob and ask for his help? If he was my soul mate, then surely I'd be able to convince him to come to my rescue. But hadn't I just told Lorelei we each needed to be our own knight in shining armor?

Something else stopped me from calling Bob. I had the distinct feeling that I'd been led through each lifetime for a specific reason. The first was to resolve my issues with my mother and let go of the past. The second timeline showed me what the future could be if I simply let down my guard and allowed myself to be loved.

But what about this one? I could see a pattern beginning to emerge. If not for Bob or my mother, then why was I here? Every instinct I had pointed to Parker—I still couldn't think of him any other way. I suspected that he was the one I needed to focus on right now. I wasn't quite sure if it was for his sake or mine.

———

A kind-faced orderly peeked into my room. "You have a guest, Ms. Hall."

Cassie!

I rushed to the visitor's lounge, hoping to see my sister, but was disappointed to see my father there instead. "Dad?"

He turned and gazed at me with pity. "Jenna." He held out his arms. "How are you today?"

I stood there, unsure what was expected of me. He held his arms out for a moment longer, then let them fall. The expression on his face was of one who expected rejection and wasn't surprised by it.

I walked toward him and took a seat on a faded couch, patting the cushion beside me. My father sat with a mournful sigh. He reached for my hand and turned it wrist upward. Bandages covered the wounds but couldn't hide the shame.

"I'm sorry," I said. Even though it wasn't mine to claim, I could see the pain in his eyes and realized how much effort it had taken him to come here.

"No, I'm the one who should be sorry," he said. "I wasn't a very good father to you girls. After your mother died, I just gave up.

Guess I blamed myself. It was easier to drink than remember her the last time I saw her."

"Dad . . ."

"No," he said. "Let me get this out. I came all the way here to tell you I'm sorry. I wish I could do things differently, but I can't. I can only go on from here and hope you'll forgive me. You and your sister both."

"I do, Dad. I do." I wrapped my arms around him and rested my head on his shoulder. At first he held me loosely, then his arms tightened until I could feel his heart beating against mine. Forgiveness came easily. If there was one thing I'd learned, it was that it was easier to forgive someone else than it was to forgive yourself. But you had to do the first to achieve the second.

Back in my room that evening, I pondered my dilemma. I needed to get to the secret room in the House of Cry to find my way back to my own reality. But how could I leave while ensuring that this *me*—the one that belonged here—stayed and got the help she needed? The only way I could think of was to convince Parker to take me to the house temporarily. Then when I'd moved on, he'd be there to make sure my counterpart safely returned to the recovery center, where he could give her the help she needed.

There was something else I could do while I waited for Parker to take me seriously. I realized that no matter which timeline I followed, there was one other constant. I always kept a journal. Why should this timeline be any different?

I was overcome with the urge to leave a piece of myself behind. I realized that I wasn't the only one who was lost. Whoever belonged in this body, this world, this reality, was lost as well. If I somehow found my way back to my own world, the least I could do was to leave a clue for whoever took back this life when I left it behind. And if somehow I never found my way back home, then at least I'd have these words to mark my passage, as the memories of the life I left behind became dimmer with time.

I searched the small room. There weren't many places to hide anything. Sure enough, I found a dime-store composition book tucked into the drawer of my nightstand. I glanced through the pages, which were mostly blank. The written pages began on the day I was admitted. Apparently my regular journal had been left behind, and I'd had to make do with this instead.

To my surprise, I found poetry. Not the sugar-sweet poems I'd found in the world where I was married to Bob, or my mother's tortured words that scraped raw nerves, but something in between. They were an almost perfect marriage of darkness and light that seemed to tap into the deepest corners of my soul. Most were unfinished, some only a few lines, but they all felt familiar, as if they'd come from deep within my own subconscious.

I lost myself in the pages of the journal, relishing the words like they were my own. And in many ways, they were. Every now and then something resonated, as if binding together our two lives, our separate experiences.

> *I saw her floating above the bay*
> *In a dress spun of shadows and silk*
> *She touched her lips and looked my way*
> *And sent me a thought on a breeze*
> *"She's coming, she's coming, take heed."*

Could the woman in this poem be Maya? Perhaps my doppelganger had sensed Maya's presence on a subconscious level, where all dreams and poems are born. And who was coming? Did the final line of the poem refer to me?

I thumbed through the pages, sometimes forgetting I hadn't written the words myself. One playful snippet seemed to sum up exactly what I'd been going through since that fateful day when I'd first entered the House of Cry.

> *Where am I going?*
> *Where have I been?*
> *In the land of me and mine*

I ran my fingers over the page. That was me, all right. Lost in the land of me and mine.

As I read farther into the journal, I realized that my alter ego had already begun her journey toward self-healing. Her writing showed that she was remorseful and grateful to be alive. She'd been eagerly participating in her therapy sessions and anxious to make it up to Cassie for the grief she'd caused. She'd even encouraged Lorelei to start chronicling her own journey to facilitate her recovery process.

I was confident that my other self would be fine once I moved on. Just in case, I added another entry for her to find when she was once more in control of her own body.

> *Had another good session with Dr. Cody. My memory has been spotty, but I trust him to help me continue my journey toward complete mental and physical healing. Worked with Lorelei today and encouraged her to continue journaling her feelings. I know it's been helpful for me and will be good for her as well. Maybe when we're out of here the two of us can continue working together. She has a real aptitude for writing that I'd like to help her develop. I hope to see Cassie tomorrow. Maybe she'll forgive me for what I've put her through.*
>
> *I've learned that the past doesn't define me. I have to let go of the blame and make my life the best it can be from this point forward. Instead of running from death, start running toward life.*

I put the pen down and sat back, realizing that while I'd started out writing for the owner of this journal, I'd ended up counseling myself as well. Maybe this was something we both needed to remember. I hoped when she read those words they would mean as much to her as they did to me.

The next morning I went into my session with Parker hoping he would confirm everything I'd told him and welcome me with open arms. That wasn't the case.

"What did you find out?" I asked.

"Have a seat," he said, pointedly ignoring my question. "First I'd like to hear more about these other personalities."

I had to be careful. I didn't want my own brother labeling me with dissociative identity disorder. "Not other personalities," I said. "One personality. One life that branches off into multiple directions. I'm Jenna Hall in each of those parallel realities, simply living a life formed by the choices I've made."

I kept my voice calm. It wouldn't do to act hysterical, no matter how frustrating it was not being able to convince him. "It wasn't easy for me to understand either, as you can imagine. And I'm still not sure exactly why I was given this opportunity, but it seems like there's a lesson to be learned with each shift in reality."

He nodded thoughtfully. I could see that something had changed. Maybe he'd done some research on that many-worlds theory he'd told me about and was starting to take me seriously. Or half seriously.

The thing was, I didn't really need him to believe me fully. I simply needed him to believe me enough to unlock the secrets of his birth and reunite with his sisters in this timeline. I'd take care of reuniting with him in my own timeline, assuming I could convince him to help me get back.

I left my session feeling more hopeful than I had yesterday. From what I knew of Parker, he was governed more by logic than imagination. But he was still my mother's son, and some of her open-mindedness had to reside in him somewhere. Given enough time, I was sure I could tap into that vein. The problem was that I had a feeling time might be running out.

I waited the rest of the morning for Cassie to arrive, searching for her face each time the door opened. I paced the room, willing her to show up. I missed her desperately. I glanced out the window for the millionth time and noticed Lorelei walking outside with a guest. My heart skittered. There was something familiar about the man walking beside her. But it couldn't be. Could it?

As they came closer, I got a better look at Lorelei's companion. It was Bob. How? Why? Was it just a coincidence? Surely if he knew Lorelei, I'd have known, wouldn't I? I twisted the ring on my fingers. Maybe not. I'd only been with him a few short weeks, hardly long enough to meet every person we knew.

Unless . . .

I tried to remember everything Bob had said about his brother. They'd had a child, a daughter. Had he mentioned a name? I couldn't remember. Could this be the niece he'd spoken about? The one I'd taken under my wing when her parents were killed? That might explain why I felt so protective of Lorelei even though we'd just met.

I followed their progress, my heart beating faster as they drew closer. A thousand sensory memories bombarded me—the clean smell of his hair, the heat of his skin against mine, the softness of his lips, and the hardness of his body. How was it possible that he was a stranger to me in this life when I knew him so well?

I wanted to run to him, to throw myself into his arms, but I realized how crazy that would seem. It didn't stop me from leaning toward the window, wishing he'd look up at me with a smile of recognition.

I tried to make myself invisible in the corner as they came into the room, afraid that I'd give myself away.

"There you are," Lorelei called, dragging Bob by the arm. "This is Jenna," she said, "the lady I told you about."

She turned to me. "Jenna, this is my uncle Bob. He's one of the good guys."

I held out my hand, my voice barely a whisper as my heart pounded in my throat. "It's nice to meet you."

His hand closed around mine in a way that was so familiar it nearly broke my heart. In another life those hands knew me intimately, had given me both comfort and pleasure. "Laura has told me so much about you."

"Laura?"

He glanced at his niece and gave her a conspirator's smile. "I mean Lorelei."

Obviously Lorelei had insisted on changing her name to something a little more exotic. I found Bob's willingness to go along with her endearing.

"She said you've been helping her get in touch with her feelings."

"Big deal," Lorelei said with a bravado that I was already beginning to realize masked her vulnerability. "She showed me how to write in a journal. That doesn't make her a saint or nothing."

Bob gave Lorelei a gentle hug. She rolled her eyes, but I could see that she adored him and he adored her as well.

"I have to admit I have a soft spot for your niece," I said. "God only knows why. She's moody, belligerent, and a pain in the ass sometimes."

"Oh, so you do know her pretty well," Bob said with a chuckle.

Lorelei punched him on the arm and stuck her tongue out at me. "Takes one to know one," she said, then threw her arms around me and gave me a quick hug.

I really did care for her, and now I understood that she was another connection in this life line. All the puzzle pieces were falling into place. Lorelei was my link to Bob in this life, and Bob would be the conduit to Lorelei in the next. Once I made that connection, I'd be able to give Lorelei the time and attention she needed to heal completely. Maybe this time it would be easier for both of us.

I left Bob and Lorelei alone to continue their visit. It was difficult to be so close to Bob and not touch him or send him meaningful glances. It wasn't time for me to insert myself into his world. Not yet. But I knew that time would come and we'd all be better for it.

I turned and caught Bob staring after me with a puzzled frown on his face. Maybe on some level he knew me. That thought gave me hope that no matter how or when, we'd always find each other again, just as I'd promised.

That afternoon I took my journal and walked alone into the woods. It was peaceful and serene, and I felt comfortable in my own skin for the first time I could remember. I found it ironic that I'd finally found my center of sanity in a place that sheltered people who struggled to hold onto theirs. Only now that I was on solid ground could I see how dangerously close I had been to falling.

I settled on a bench beneath the shade of a lush oak. The air was fresh with the green scent of pine, reminding me of Christmases past, beribboned gifts, and delicious expectation. It sent me back to a time of innocence when anything was possible. I tipped my head back and closed my eyes. The sun was warm on my skin. The simple pleasure of fresh air and sunshine brought a smile to my face.

It wasn't long before I realized I wasn't alone. I knew, without even opening my eyes, that Maya had joined me on the bench.

I suspected she was always somewhere close by, even when she wasn't physically present.

"It's a beautiful day, isn't it?"

She murmured her assent. A comfortable silence stretched between us. I no longer felt the need to batter Maya with questions. I felt as if all the answers were inside me, simply waiting for the concealing layers to be peeled away.

"You know, when I was little I believed we all had a guardian angel over our shoulder," I said. "It was comforting to know someone was watching over me, protecting and guiding me."

"So it wouldn't surprise you if I suddenly sprouted wings?"

I had to laugh. "Somehow nothing you did would surprise me at this point."

She didn't sprout wings, just turned the question around. "When did you stop believing in guardian angels?"

"I don't know exactly. I guess about the same time I stopped believing in Santa Claus and the Easter bunny."

"And what do you believe now?"

I thought about it for a little while, remembering my chat with Lorelei. "I guess I'm beginning to believe I'm my own guardian angel. I just have to trust my instincts and listen to that inner voice that intuitively knows right from wrong. It's up to me to find my own truth."

"So maybe a guardian angel is simply a physical manifestation of your own psyche."

"Now you sound like my brother the psychiatrist." I smiled at how easily the word flowed from my lips. *My brother*. I knew that no matter what, when I returned home I was going to do whatever it took to find Parker and make him a part of my life. "He's . . ."

I turned, but Maya was gone. I glanced up and down the path. There was no sign of her in either direction. It was as if she'd simply vanished into thin air. I shook my head. I'd never get used to her ability to pop in and out of my life without even stirring a breeze.

Maybe she was right. Maybe she was simply a manifestation of my own psyche, my inner wisdom.

I picked up my notebook and began writing. I wrote about life and death and all the choices we make along the way. I wrote about the people we touch and those who touch us. The words flowed effortlessly, as if they'd been stored inside for an eternity and had finally been set free. They danced across the page with gleeful abandon. Arrows snaked between paragraphs, connecting ideas to one another. Doodles and notes adorned the margins.

Writing my thoughts down helped emphasize the ones that rang true and highlighted those that fell short. I fell into a trance-like state, unaware of the passage of time. When I was finished, I felt purified and whole.

17

The next morning I woke refreshed. I'd slept easily and dreamlessly. I ate breakfast with a gusto that even Lorelei commented on.

"You're going to get fat if you eat like that all the time," she warned me.

"Well, then I'll be fat and happy, won't I? No one will say I died regretting that I deprived myself of one last guilty pleasure."

She pointed to the plate of mile-high pancakes in front of me. "Did you know . . . ?"

I held up my hand to stop her. "If it involves body parts, I don't want to hear it. I'm enjoying my breakfast, and I'd like to keep it that way."

Lorelei eyed me suspiciously. "You've been different lately."

"That's why we're here, isn't it?"

"I guess," she said.

It wasn't a lie. I did feel different. I wasn't the same person who had been tempted to take her own life. That person was a stranger. I had a new outlook, an acceptance of who I was and who I could be. Wasn't acceptance one of the four traits I used the swan tattoo to remember?

"I'm even thinking of getting a tattoo," I said. I held out my wrist. "Right here."

"Really?" I could see the skepticism in Lorelei's eyes. I couldn't blame her. I didn't look like your typical ink enthusiast. "I'm thinking of a swan," I said.

"A swan, huh?"

"Yes, a swan." I didn't explain any further. It wasn't for anyone else to understand or approve. As long as the swan had meaning for me, that was all that mattered.

"I guess that's cool," she said, then changed the subject. "Uncle Bob asked about you."

"Oh?" I felt warmth rise to my cheeks and hoped the flush wouldn't give me away.

"I told him you were married."

"What?"

She chuckled. "Just kidding. I said you were too good for him, but if he played his cards right, you might just let him take you to dinner."

"I might just do that," I admitted.

"I have to warn you, though. He's a bit of a workaholic. That can be a problem."

"I know."

She frowned. "You know?"

I finished my pancakes, then carefully peeled a banana, avoiding her gaze. "I mean I know that can be a problem." I broke off half of the banana and handed it to Lorelei. She bit into it, still watching me with a half frown on her forehead.

"So," I said, "I guess that means he's not married?"

"Nope. He was engaged once, but that didn't work out."

I felt a stab of jealousy. What if I got back to the real world and found that Bob was already taken? What if I went through all this only to find out that the future I'd glimpsed wasn't even available? No, I was certain that Bob was waiting to find the right woman, the same way I was waiting for the right man to come along. It would happen. I'd make sure of that.

Just then I heard the opening chords of "A Thousand Nights," the song that Bob and I had danced to a lifetime ago. Up until now I hadn't even noticed the music playing softly over the loudspeakers, but hearing that song again made my chest tighten with longing. Was it coincidence that the song started playing just now or was it a sign?

I closed my eyes, feeling Bob's arms around me once again as we swayed to the music. Contentment, security, love—those feelings washed over me. If I had the chance to find love again, I knew I wouldn't take it for granted. I'd treasure every single moment.

I was so caught up in my fantasy that I almost missed Lorelei's next comment. "So what was Cassie's excuse this time?"

"Huh?" I shook my head, trying to bring myself back to this reality. "Oh, something came up," I said, avoiding Lorelei's gaze. I wasn't sure if Cassie was punishing me for abandoning her or protecting herself in case I tried to take my own life again. I knew Cassie, though. She might be hurt and angry now, but she wouldn't stay mad for long. Eventually she'd forgive me—even if it wasn't *this* me.

I felt confident that the person who'd written in the journal had learned her lesson and wouldn't disappoint Cassie again. "She'll come soon," I said. "And it'll be all right."

At least I hoped that was the case.

The thought of making amends with Cassie brought Diane to mind. I'd already vowed to apologize to her when I returned to my real world. But wasn't I in a timeline where I'd hurt her? She deserved an apology here as well.

————————

It was another hour before I was able to use the telephone, which gave me plenty of time to worry about what Diane's reaction might be. What if she hung up on me before I even had a chance to apologize?

I called the number and waited while the phone rang. My heart sank as I waited for her voice mail to pick up again. Just when I was about to give up, I heard her voice on the line.

I tried to speak, but nothing came out but a squeak. I cleared my throat and tried again. "Diane? This is Jenna. Jenna Hall."

Silence.

"Please don't hang up," I begged. "I have to tell you how sorry I am. I know what I did was unforgivable, and I wouldn't blame you if you never wanted to talk to me again, but I am truly sorry for letting you down. I was thoughtless and selfish and maybe a little jealous that you were so happy and I was so miserable. That's not an excuse but an explanation. I'm sorry. I'm so sorry. Please forgive me. I miss you."

I stopped, having run out of words. I waited. She could yell and scream and call me names. It didn't matter. I deserved it all. But the only sound on the other end of the line was a deep inhale, then a long, trembling exhale. Finally she said the words I needed to hear. "I forgive you."

It was only a start. I knew I couldn't just apologize and waltz back into her life. I'd have to earn her trust again, and who knew how long that would take. But it was a start.

"Thank you," I said. I hoped she heard the sincerity in my voice. I felt a weight lift from my heart. I knew I'd have to make this same phone call again when I returned to my own timeline, but I'd apologize a thousand times in a thousand timelines if I had to, over and over again.

When I hung up, the woman behind the desk, who couldn't have helped overhearing my conversation, nodded with silent approval.

I was still feeling optimistic when my scheduled meeting with Parker rolled around.

"Have a seat," he said. His voice was carefully controlled, but I could see something had changed.

I lowered myself onto the chair across from his desk and leaned forward. "What did you find out?"

He took a deep breath, then let it out with a soft sigh. "How did you know? I had to pull some pretty tight strings to get this information myself."

I felt a weight slide from my shoulders. It was true. Up until this moment I hadn't realized that a tiny seed of doubt had been planted in my mind. What if it had all been the product of a delusional mind? What if he'd been right about my mental illness, and every other timeline, including the one I was desperate to return to, was just the product of an unbalanced mind? The fact that he'd verified my story erased all doubt. Everything had happened exactly as I remembered.

"I told you," I said. "I met you in an alternate reality where my mother hadn't given you up for adoption and we were raised as brother and sister. I don't think we were very close, but you gave me a piece of jewelry that I wanted for my birthday, so you must have cared about me. And you were trying to help me find a job. Maybe we had some unresolved issues. Maybe this is our second chance to get to know each other as equals."

He shook his head. "I don't know about that, but according to the paperwork we do share the same mother. That would make you my half-sister, I guess."

I could see that the therapist in him didn't want to feed into my delusions, if that's what they were. But there was something in his eyes that said he didn't disbelieve me as much today as he had yesterday, and as far as I could see we were making progress.

"So where do we go from here?" Parker asked. He watched me closely.

"Well, I guess it's not really important that you believe me. I think my mission—or whatever it is—is complete now. I'm free to go back to my real life, and you can build a new relationship with your sisters, Jenna and Cassie."

"As simple as that?"

I wasn't sure, but it felt right. "Yeah, I think so."

"How do you get back to your real life?" he asked with a quick, surreptitious glance at the bandages on my wrists.

I shook my head. No, not that way. "The house," I explained. "The House of Cry. There's a secret room, and that's where it always happens. Some kind of portal or something. I don't know how or why; it's just there."

I forced myself to slow down, trying not to sound hysterical. "See, it all started when my sister and I went to look at a house. I called it the House of Cry after a poem my mother wrote. While we were there, I went into a room I hadn't seen before and . . . okay, I know this sounds crazy, but I hit my head and woke up in an alternate reality where my mother was still alive."

I could see I was losing him. "Look, it doesn't matter whether or not you believe me. I'm going to get back to the House of Cry one way or another and find my way back to my real world. What's important is that you be there when I leave."

"Why?"

"Because . . ." How could I explain? "Because I don't know what happens to the person who belongs in this life when I move on. I don't know if she'll have any memory of what happened while I was using her body, or if it'll all be a blank. Either way, she's going to need you. You're going to have to help her understand."

"And what if you don't move on? What if you're trapped here in this life?" I could see he was humoring me, but it was some-thing I'd considered as well.

"Then I'm going to need a big brother to help me deal with it."

His face softened, and he gave a barely perceptible nod. "Okay," he said. "I'll be there either way."

I couldn't believe that Parker—I still couldn't think of him any other way—had agreed to accompany me. Maybe he could see that I was determined to go one way or the other and knew that I'd be safer if he was with me. Maybe this was part of our therapy, and he thought that confronting my fantasy would lead to a breakthrough. Or maybe some small part of him believed me. Either way, I was grateful.

He had only one request. He wanted to stop at the grave of the mother he'd never met.

I was unprepared for the emotional impact of leaving the recovery center with Parker. I trembled with a combination of excitement and fear of the unknown, like a child leaving for the first day of school. As much as I wanted to move on, I was leaving safety and security behind me. Had I done enough? Would Lorelei continue with her journals? Would Cassie forgive me?

I stopped and turned to Parker. "Would you do me another favor?"

"What's that?" he asked.

"Even if you don't believe my story about alternate realities, you know I was right about the fact that we share a mother."

He nodded.

"No matter what, you're still my brother," I said. "Cassie and I need you. And I think you also need us. Promise you'll stay in our lives now that we've found each other?"

He took my hand and gave it a gentle squeeze. "I promise," he said.

That was all I needed to hear. I felt like I'd accomplished everything I was meant to do in this timeline and looked forward to moving on to what I was sure would be the world where I belonged.

I led Parker to the grave site tucked into a quiet corner of the cemetery and pointed out the slab of granite with my mother's name carved into the stone—Marjorie Parker Hall. I took a long, quivering breath. It looked exactly as it had the day I'd stood in this very spot on the morning of my birthday.

Parker wasn't surprised by the votives, cards, and letters littering her grave. I'd explained about the constant stream of admirers who visited our mother's grave. He was curious, however, turning items over, reading bits of poetry and personal notes left behind. I only had eyes for one thing on my mother's grave, however.

A purple iris.

While Parker got down on his knees and said a prayer for the mother he had never known, I ran my finger over the velvety petals. Cassie had been here. She always left a single purple iris on our mother's grave. She said the iris was symbolic of both sorrow and hope. Cassie had read that according to tradition, an iris placed on a woman's grave would summon the goddess Iris, who would guide her soul to eternity.

It was only now that I realized the iris was Cassie's way of saying she forgave our mother. Why couldn't I? I had held onto my anger and resentment for so long, and it only hurt myself.

It was too late to tell my mother that I understood. I understood why she'd kept secrets that haunted her, why she'd turned that regret into self-hatred, and why she finally couldn't face another day of living with the wrong choices. I understood that she lived with guilt even though she'd made the choices she had for all the right reasons. I understood and I forgave her.

Letting go released an emotional weight from my shoulders. I could forgive her now, knowing this was only one of many paths she'd chosen. I mouthed a silent prayer, knowing that in some of those lifetimes she'd found the peace and happiness she'd been unable to find in this one.

I took the flower and brought it to my face, inhaling the subtle scent. Sorrow and hope. I'd had my share of both emotions these last few weeks. Overshadowing them both, however, was a new sense of anticipation. It was time to go home. I was so close to my own reality that I could sense it waiting for me right around the corner. All I had to do was step inside the secret room and I'd be there.

"What was she like?" Parker asked.

For a moment I wasn't sure how to answer him. There was the emotionally absent mother of my childhood memories and the carefree mother I'd recently discovered. Which one was real—the darkness or the light? I suspected the truth was somewhere in between.

"She was . . ." I searched his eyes, seeing remnants of the little boy who wondered who his mommy was. "She was a woman who felt things deeply. It was both a blessing and a curse. I do know she loved you. When she lost you, she lost a piece of herself, and she was never whole again."

I wasn't sure if that helped him or not. His eyes were bright and his voice thick with unshed tears. He pressed his fingers to his lips, then traced her name on the cold stone and whispered something to the mother he had never known.

I turned away, feeling like an intruder on his private grief. After a few moments, he stood and brushed the dirt from his pants. "Let's go," he said in a gruff voice that no longer betrayed emotion.

I nodded. As much as I wanted to tell him about the mother he never knew, it wouldn't bring her back. In his world she'd been dead for most of his life. Hearing about the mother who'd raised him in another reality would only hurt him more.

He followed my directions, his gaze trained on the road. I wondered if he was afraid to let me see the yearning in his eyes. Maybe he was afraid that if he let himself believe other realities existed, he'd finally realize all he'd lost in this one.

"There," I said, pointing out the road leading to the House of Cry. I watched as we turned off the main road, my heart in my throat. *Almost there. Almost home.* I leaned forward as we rounded the bend. "Right there," I said, pointing excitedly.

But I was pointing at nothing. The spot where the house should have stood was empty. I looked to the left and right, frantically searching for the house I knew should have been standing right in front of us.

"Where?" Parker asked.

The air seeped from my lungs in a slow escape, leaving me limp and deflated. "It should be right there," I said, refusing to believe my eyes. Parker slowed to a stop and turned to look at me. The doubt on his face barely registered. All I could think about was that the house, along with the secret room and the only doorway back to my own reality, was gone. Vanished.

Parker put the car in park and turned, angling his body toward me. My brother was gone, and the therapist had returned. "Now are you ready to face reality?"

"No," I screamed. "This isn't my reality." I pointed out the open window: "My reality is out there."

"There's nothing there," he said, pointing out the obvious.

"Maybe we took a wrong turn," I said, grasping at straws. "Maybe we . . ." Then I saw it, the nearly hidden path riddled with weeds that was as familiar to me as my own name. "There," I said, grasping the door handle. "There's the path."

I jumped out of the car and raced up the barely perceptible path to where the front door should have been. Only then did I see the charred foundation, the burned-out ashes and blackened remnants of what used to be.

I dropped to my knees. "No, no, no."

18

Parker was there, lifting me back to my feet. I broke through the paralysis gripping me and stumbled forward, shaking my head in denial.

"It was right here," I cried. I stood where the kitchen would have been, seeing it clearly in my memory. This was where my mother had baked me a cake and wished me happy birthday as if she'd been there for every birthday in the last twenty years. This was where I'd finally filled the empty void where my mother should have been.

I moved forward, tracing my footsteps through the ruined dirt to where the living room would be, where Parker had given me a pin that looked like the tree of life. That gift represented everything I'd come to learn about the many divergent paths we live, teaching me that the present is only an illusion leading to many possibilities where the branches diverged. It was up to us to make each path the best choice possible, despite the obstacles thrown in our way.

And here were the remnants of the bedroom where Bob had made love to me and shown me what was possible if I only opened up and allowed myself to take the risk of being hurt again. Every choice involved risk. If we loved others, they had the power to hurt us by leaving or dying. But without love, what was the sense of any of it? The alternative was a lonely heart that withered and died.

It was all here—my past, my present, and my future, all here in the charred rubble of the House of Cry. I walked deeper, aware of

Parker standing on the sidelines watching cautiously. There was something here. I felt it. Something I had yet to understand.

I searched frantically for where the secret room might be. If I could only pinpoint its location, maybe there was hope after all. If not, I was doomed to remain here in this life with only the scars on my wrist to remind me of the mistakes I'd made.

I scoured the dry and ruined landscape, trying to remember where I was when I'd entered the secret room. Here? Or here? I was only vaguely aware of Parker calling my name as I circled round and round and round. Tears blurred my vision. I moved without conscious thought, letting instinct guide me.

Then it happened. I felt the familiar vertigo and welcomed the sense of déjà vu that overtook my senses. A tight white vortex sucked me inward, and the world seemed to spin and dissolve around me. I could see Parker's face, his eyes concerned. His arms reached out, out, out, too late to catch me as I began to fall.

———————

There was no slip into unconsciousness this time. One moment I was outside with Parker and the next I was back in the secret room. I shook off the dizziness and reached for the door, convinced my real life was waiting for me on the other side. I turned the handle and opened the door to find . . . another hallway lined with a series of unopened doors.

What the hell?

I spun around, reached for the door behind me, and opened it again, only to find another hallway lined with even more doors. I threw open one, then another, trapped in a never-ending labyrinth of doors. Which one to choose?

My breath came in short, quick bursts, and a throbbing pulse pounded in my temples. I knew I was running out of time. I had to find my way out. If I didn't, I'd be lost forever.

I stood frozen with indecision, looking around me. The hallways stretched endlessly in every direction, lined with almost identical doors. Almost. They all looked the same at first glance, but there were miniscule variations. In some cases it was barely enough to tell them apart . . . a curlicue engraved here, a shade lighter wood there, a glass knob on one, and a metal handle on another.

Pick one, pick one. More hallways. More doors. How would I ever find my way out? Shifting shadows raced ahead of me, shadows that twisted and turned and disappeared just out of reach. Here. Then there. *Maya?* Was she trying to lead me to the right portal? I ran, trying to keep up with the fleeting shadow that slipped in and out of my sight.

Finally I reached a dead end. Only one choice was left. I threw open the final door and found myself in a dimly-lit room. There was Cassie at the far end, her back to me. I recognized her hair, the butter yellow array of curls that had a mind of their own. "Cassie," I cried, but my voice was small and muffled. I ran across the room, calling her name, but she didn't move.

Only then did I notice that she was kneeling at the side of a casket.

I slowed. Something told me I didn't want to see inside the casket. I looked around and noticed a few other people here and there. No one seemed to notice me. At the back of the room I saw Maya sitting alone, a dark veil pulled over her face.

I turned from Maya to Cassie and back again, shaking my head. It couldn't be. I had to see for myself.

"Cassie?" I stepped closer, trying desperately to get her attention, but to no avail. The walk across the room seemed to take forever. It was as if I were pushing against a wall of cold, stale air. Cassie knelt beside the casket, sobbing like her heart was broken. I looked over her shoulder, somehow not surprised to see the body nestled on white satin inside the rosewood casket.

It didn't even look like me. It looked like a wax figure carved by someone who barely knew me. The hair was wrong, the absence of life horrifyingly real. I saw the purple iris nestled in my cold, clasped hands.

I was wrong. So wrong. I'd thought there were only two paths leading from each choice, but sometimes there were multiple outcomes diverging from a single choice. Only now did I realize that if there was a reality where I'd attempted suicide and failed, then logically there'd be an alternate reality where I'd attempted suicide and succeeded. That's where I was now, a ghost walking in a world where I no longer existed.

"I'm sorry, Cassie," I said. My voice was a hollow whisper that floated beyond her reach. She couldn't hear me, but a shiver rocked her shoulders. She'd never know how much I regretted hurting her this way.

"How could you do this?" Cassie sobbed. "You broke your promise. You said you'd never leave."

There was more pain than anger in her voice. I wanted to reach out and comfort her, but it was too late. I no longer had the right to comfort or explain. I'd thrown it all away when I'd taken my own life. I felt a deep disappointment in myself for wasting something so precious. I glanced at Maya sitting at the back of the room. She held my gaze.

I blinked, but there were no tears on my cheeks. Ghosts don't cry.

I turned my back on the sad coffin and walked toward Maya, noticing again how few people were here to give their respects: my sister and father, as well as a few coworkers from the bar. The lack of mourners was in stark contrast to all the friends surrounding me when I'd been married to Bob. Only now did I realize how barren my life had become, how few people I'd let inside.

If I had another chance at life, I'd change that. I'd reach out and be a friend to others, and accept their friendship in return. I wouldn't push away people who mattered for a past that no longer did. I'd come out of my lonely shell and experience everything this wondrous life had to offer. If only I had another chance.

I noticed Diane standing in the doorway. She started to come inside, then stopped and shook her head, sadness and regret etched across her face. I reached out, knowing I couldn't touch her. She turned and walked away. It was too late. I'd never be able to apologize or renew our friendship. She'd spend the rest of her life wondering why I'd betrayed our friendship when she'd needed me most.

Cassie's voice drew my attention. I turned and saw her addressing the room. "This is one of my mother's poems," she said. "Jenna had it in her hand when she died, so it must have been important to her."

I closed my eyes, knowing exactly what poem she was going to read.

It was too much. I'd been through so much, only to find myself in the place where I always feared I'd end up. I found my way to the row of seats where Maya waited. I sat beside her, ashamed to meet her gaze. "I failed," I murmured.

She reached out and closed her hand over mine. "There is no failure, only branches that have been prematurely pruned and some that have withered and died. But there are other branches that will spread out and reach full maturity."

"What happens when they're all dead?"

She tipped her head and gave me a mysterious smile. "Then you have a full life spectrum to look back on. Every choice, every single outcome will have been experienced. There would be no regrets and no road left untraveled."

"But why don't I remember them all now?"

"You could if you tried hard enough. But your brain has been taught to follow memories in a linear path rather than a circular one."

I nodded. She was simply confirming everything I'd come to understand. Our lives consist of every choice ever made. Success and failure exist simultaneously, and we live with the consequences of both choices.

I thought back to my conversation with Lorelei and realized I'd been wrong to imply there was only one end to turning your life around. Death didn't necessarily mean it was too late. Even if we were stupid enough to try to end our lives, we still would have a second chance to get it right. That wasn't true only for myself, but for my mother as well. We don't lose people; they are simply moving along parallel paths.

"I don't care about the other choices," I said, my voice quivering. "I just want to get back to the life I remember living. There's so much more I understand now. So much more I want to do." I glanced back at my sister. "I want to keep the promise I made to Cassie. I swore I'd never leave her."

I was embarrassed by the whine in my voice. If being dead hadn't taught me a lesson, then nothing would. I straightened my spine. "I have to get back to the secret room somehow. I have to find my way back."

"You don't need the house or the secret room," Maya said. "They were simply symbols that allowed your mind to travel in a nonlinear fashion. The power was inside you all along."

I glanced at Cassie, not surprised to see the old figurine clutched in her hand. "Like Dorothy?"

Maya nodded.

"So what do I do now? Click my heels and repeat, 'There's no place like home'?"

"You could," she said. "Or you could simply close your eyes, concentrate, feel the flow of your life, and choose the path where you want to be."

"Seriously?"

"Try it."

I closed my eyes and took a slow, deep breath. I tried to relax, but felt my concentration being pulled in different directions. My mind jumped from one idea to the next. The harder I tried to find my way home, the more it eluded me.

I opened my eyes, about to ask Maya for more guidance, but she was gone. Everyone was gone. The room was empty. Shadows were forming in the corners, lifting and spreading and threatening to overtake the entire room. I knew I had to leave *now*.

I closed my eyes, took a deep breath, and let go as I exhaled. I stopped fighting and let myself sink deeper and deeper, letting go a little more with each breath. I stopped struggling, and as soon as I stopped trying to find it, the magic found me. I felt my consciousness pulled and lifted, setting me adrift along the flowing life stream.

A voice whispered through my consciousness. It might have been my own but seemed to come from a different place, farther back and to the right. *It's time to go deep, time to find the secret room inside you, always so tantalizing and just out of reach. Delve deep. Open your mind. Listen with your heart and embrace the knowledge.*

I had no sense of time or place, only a vast, infinite space. The temptation to simply let go and float forever was so great I almost forgot my mission—to get back to Cassie and the timeline in which I belonged. I had to resist the siren call of this infinite in-between and find my way back to Cassie. I focused on the sound of her voice, her sweet smile. Over and over I repeated the promise I'd made, holding the promise tight like a lifeline. "I'll never leave you, Cassie. I'll never leave you all alonely."

When I opened my eyes, I was in my own bedroom. Everything slipped into place, like pieces of a puzzle. I didn't have to ask. I knew I was home.

My heart swelled with gratitude. Although I'd tried to make things right in other timelines, this was where I truly belonged.

My life wasn't perfect, but it fit me comfortably, like a well-worn pair of slippers. This was where I had things to do: apologies to make and promises to keep.

The room was the same as I'd left it but with subtle differences, as if a thoughtful houseguest had used it temporarily and put it back almost exactly the same. A notebook lay open on the table—brand new, pristine, and seductive. I brushed my fingers across the smooth surface.

I'd always blamed writing for my mother's breakdown. It was as if the words were cancer cells rapidly multiplying into deadly tumors. I could see now that her dark poetry was a symptom rather than the cause of her depression.

There was no need for me to fear the blank pages spread out before me. Writing couldn't hurt me. It certainly couldn't kill me. If anything, it just might save me.

I started slowly, hesitantly. One simple word followed by another, soon gaining speed until they began tumbling one after another in a slanting, downhill avalanche. I wrote about everything I could remember up to finding the House of Cry. Then I wrote about everything that had happened since. I didn't want to forget a single thing.

My childhood home was a place of bricks and dreams and long hallways to nowhere. A place where memories fell softly around fragile shoulders in billowing waves of sadness. Alone. Alone with my thoughts, alone with my shattered dreams, alone with my blood-spattered grief. Eventually I found myself recovering from a breakdown in comfort and solitude. And then I lost myself completely, one slender branch pruned before it could fully blossom.

What I learned most of all is that the journey is inside us. To fully live our lives, we have to follow every conceivable path, experience the outcome of each choice, the here and not-here, the now and not-now. Each choice has its own destination, from beginning to end, and each choice has a lesson to be learned. This is the path I choose. I know that the memories will fade, and soon the other realities will feel like a dream, but the lessons I've learned will stay with me always. It doesn't matter which path we find ourselves walking, for they all lead to the same place—a life fully lived, with every opportunity experienced and every doorway opened and explored.

As it turns out, I was never really lost. I know there are other realities where my life is different, but this is the one I chose to be conscious. This is the one where I'm needed and where I need to be.

The Doorway to Everwhen lies within each one of us.

I don't know exactly when I started crying. By the time I noticed the ink running with tears, my cheeks were wet, my eyes swollen. They were painless tears, however. Cleansing tears.

19

My keys were hanging by the door, where I always kept them. Who knew I'd be so happy to see something as simple as my own car keys? I jumped in the car and drove to the one place I needed to see with my own eyes before I could be sure I was back where I belonged.

I made my way to the House of Cry, nearly weeping with joy when I saw it standing undamaged and whole right where I remembered. It was unoccupied but hardly felt empty. If anything, it seemed to be brimming with life. It wore the fading sunlight like a soft cloak, glowing with promise. The only thing missing from this picture was me.

The for-sale sign leaned crookedly along the tree-lined path. My heart skipped a beat when I saw Bob's picture in the corner above the realtor's logo. The house wouldn't be on the market for long. The house, like Bob, was meant to be mine, and I'd do whatever I needed to make sure it happened.

I wrapped my arms around myself and twirled like a schoolgirl. Everything was going to be all right. No, not just all right. It was going to be wonderful. I stretched my arms out and raised my face to the sky. The setting sun painted the sky in shades of sherbet. Branches touched and intertwined, forming a living canopy overhead.

Buying the house was only one of the many things on my mental to-do list. I intended to keep my promise to Cassie and let her know I'd never let her down. I'd find Parker and make him part of our lives. I'd make amends with Diane before it was too late. Most of all, I'd take the initiative and ask Bob out on a date. He had no idea that he was about to find his soul mate.

I had one more stop to make before then, however.

There's a moment just before dusk when the light angles just right, shimmering through the air and turning colors into a surreal tableau somehow brighter, more vivid, more alive, like an alternate universe seen through a fragile curtain laid over our own. It's a teasing light, taunting us with the knowledge that no matter how perfect our reality, there's something waiting just beyond our visions, forever out of reach and only glimpsed by accident.

I made my way through the cemetery, seeing the graves with a new sense of understanding. Philosophers, theologians, scientists, and mathematicians all try to make it so complicated, when the answer is simplicity itself. We are, we were, we always will be. Every choice exists and every possibility is experienced until the final branch is pruned.

I stopped at the weeping angel monument. Every time I'd passed this spot I'd been overcome by the sense of loss for a life cut tragically short. Now I smiled knowing that little Addie Rose lived on in a myriad of alternate realities. She'd live and laugh and love over many lifetimes.

I moved on and stepped reverently toward my mother's grave. The poignant notes and messages left behind filled me with hope rather than sadness. My mother's life hadn't been wasted. Even in death she managed to touch and inspire people. I felt a sense of peace knowing that she lived on, both here and in other worlds.

I knelt on the ground. "I miss you, Mom," I said, remembering both the woman my childhood memory had colored with black crayons and the one brimming with light whom I'd known for only a short while. "I miss the woman you were and the woman you could have been," I said.

I traced her name on the cool stone, *Marjorie Parker Hall*, focusing long and hard on her middle name. "I'll find him again," I promised her. "I'll find Parker and make him part of our family. We'll all be together, just like you wanted."

I bent my head in prayer, noticing the paper fluttering beneath a rock. I knew even before reading it what I'd find. It was my mother's poem. I read it again with a new understanding, hearing my sister's voice as she read the poignant lines at my funeral.

HOUSE OF CRY

From six pounds of squalling meat
To six pounds of stone-cold ash
How do you measure a man's life between
Do you count the people he loved
Or those who loved him in return
Is it measured in kisses or tears
By peace or pain or candle prayers
Is it valued for the lives touched along the way
Or nothing more than the measure of time
Lived and died in the House of Cry

The words spoke to me now in a way they hadn't before. I felt closer to my mother, with a better understanding of her pain and sorrow, her hopes and dreams. Had she made this same journey through the House of Cry? If so, had it finally brought her the peace and understanding she craved? Had she seen me grow to womanhood, cradled her grandchildren, and found new loves along each path?

I placed the poem back beneath the rock. Maybe it would hold meaning for someone else who traveled this way.

My reverie was broken by a familiar voice.

"I was wondering when you'd get here."

It was Maya, but she was nowhere in sight. The voice came from somewhere inside me. I smiled with understanding. She'd given me the clues, hadn't she? I simply hadn't understood at the time.

Like the secret room, Maya was simply a physical manifestation of my higher consciousness, the voice that lived inside my own mind. All I had to do was listen with an open heart, and she'd be there whenever I needed her guidance.

"I'm here now," I whispered to the wind. And I was, finally. Fully and completely here. "Thank you."

I knew this part of my journey was over. I'd seen my life through a series of choices and realized that I couldn't blame anyone else for my own sadness—not my mother, my father, my sister or brother. I was the only one responsible for my unhappiness.

That realization should have been depressing, but it wasn't. If the only person to blame for my unhappiness was me, then conversely I was the one person who could change it. I had the power to choose whether to be happy or to dwell in misery. I controlled my own destiny.

I knew that the rest of the journey was still ahead of me. There would be times when I stumbled along the way. Life was full of choices—some right, some wrong—but there's something to be learned from each of them.

I pressed a kiss to the cool stone, saying my final goodbye. My days of mourning were over. From now on I'd make the most of each day and enjoy it to the fullest.

I stood with new determination to make my life the best it could be. Before I could turn from my mother's grave, however, a new voice broke the silence, one I recognized like my own.

"Here you are."

Cassie. My heart leaped. As I turned to hug her, my mind journeyed back to that long-ago day when she'd found me here at the cemetery and said those exact same words. But the person I was today was so different from the one she'd found here then.

I wrapped my arms around her and held her close. I couldn't help the words that tumbled out of my mouth as I held her tight. "Oh, Cassie, I've missed you so much."

She held my hug for a beat longer than expected before pulling away. "Yeah, because dinner last night was so long ago." She rolled her eyes. "What's up with you? You've been acting strange the last few weeks."

"I have?"

"Well, stranger than normal."

The smile seemed to start at my toes and work its way through my entire body. Now I knew I was home.

"I have so much to tell you," I said. I wasn't sure how much of my story I'd tell Cassie. Maybe the changes she saw in me would be enough, regardless of how or why I got there.

She took my hand. "Well, you can tell me on the way to the realtor's office. We're going to be late."

"Late?"

"Yeah, we're making an offer on the house today. Did you forget?"

I shook my head, realizing that everything was falling into place exactly as it was meant to be. "No, I didn't forget. I just lost track of time."

"Are you sure you don't want to touch up your makeup?" Cassie asked, giving me a light jab. "Bob is going to be there, and I've seen the way you two have been looking at each other."

I felt a warm flush creep to my cheeks. I couldn't wait to see him, but I knew if we hadn't initially met that day at the House of Cry, we'd have run into each other somewhere else. Nothing is predestined, but opportunities show up every day. It's simply a matter of choosing whether or not to take advantage of them.

"I'll touch up my makeup in the car."

We stood side by side. I glanced back one more time at my mother's grave, feeling a sense of peace. I wanted to tell her that everything was going to be all right, but I knew that on some level she already knew.

"Bob's pretty sure they'll accept our offer," Cassie said.

"They'll accept," I assured her. "The House of Cry was meant to be ours."

"House of what?"

I almost repeated myself but stopped. Somehow the phrase no longer fit. There would be no tears here, only happiness. The House of Cry, like the lessons I'd learned along the way, was part of my past now. From this moment forward, I'd move toward the future.

"Are you coming?" Cassie asked.

"Yeah," I said, reaching into my pocket and feeling the items I'd brought from the house. "I just have to do one more thing. Wait for me in the car, okay?"

She gave me an unreadable look, then turned and walked away.

I knelt down and dug a channel in the dirt at the head of my mother's grave. "In the graveyard where they belong, Mom," I whispered, then placed a black crayon into the shallow depression. I swept a handful of dirt over the top and patted it gently, burying all the darkness I'd been hanging onto most of my life.

Somehow I knew my mother would approve.

20

One Year Later

Sunshine streamed through the kitchen window, carrying the promise of spring in the air. Jenna sat at the table enjoying a second cup of coffee and a few moments of peace and quiet. It was hard to believe how far she'd come in one short year. It wasn't that long ago that she had sought out solitude. Now it was a rare commodity. She preferred it that way.

Cassie stumbled out of her bedroom and sniffed the air. "Something smells fabulous."

"Roast duck. It's my new favorite meal."

"If it tastes as good as it smells," Cassie said, peeking into the oven, "it'll be my new favorite, too."

"Then I'll make one for your birthday as well."

Cassie frowned, then glanced around the kitchen. "Where did you get a duck?"

"At the market this morning." Jenna raised one eyebrow pointedly. "Some of us manage to climb out of bed before noon."

Cassie crossed the room and gave her sister a hug. "And some of us look forward to being able to sleep in on the weekend."

Jenna lifted her cup and pointed it at the counter. "There's more coffee in the pot."

Cassie rubbed her eyes, stretched, and yawned. She trudged to the counter, poured herself a cup of coffee, and joined Jenna at the table. "Why are you so chipper this morning?"

"Just feeling good." Jenna took a deep breath. She had so much to be thankful for. "It's going to be a great day."

"Sure is." Cassie said. She reached out and brushed her fingers through Jenna's hair. "I'm glad you decided to go back to your natural color. It makes you look younger. Softer."

After all this time, it still felt good to have her sister's approval. Jenna knew it wasn't just her hair, though. Looking back at pictures from a year ago, she almost didn't recognize the woman looking back. She was thinner then, almost gaunt, as if she didn't deserve the comfort of food. And a deep reservoir of sadness cast shadows in her eyes.

Cassie snapped her fingers. "Speaking of birthdays . . ." She snatched her purse from across the table, reached inside, then pulled out a wrapped box. "I thought I'd give you my gift before everyone else arrives."

Jenna opened the package slowly. She already knew what she'd find inside the box. When the final bit of wrapping paper and ribbon fell to the floor, she unwound the tissue paper to find a brand-new, bright and shiny porcelain Dorothy figurine.

She shot Cassie a puzzled glance. "What happened to the old one?"

Cassie shrugged. "Don't know. I couldn't find it and figured maybe it was time for a replacement. New Dorothy, new year, new beginnings."

Yes, Jenna thought. *New beginnings.*

She placed the figurine in the center of the table, where she'd see it all day. "There's no place like home," she murmured. As she said the words, ghostly fingers walked up and down her spine.

"Speaking of home, " Cassie said. "I suppose you'll be moving out soon, huh?"

Jenna nodded. "Yes, but luckily my fiancé is a realtor. He has his eye on a great place to start that bed-and-breakfast he's always wanted."

Cassie gave her a hug. "I'm gonna miss you, Sis. This past year has seen a lot of changes, but the best has been living here with you."

"It has," Jenna agreed. "But like you said, new beginnings, right?"

"That's right. Now I'd better get dressed before people start arriving.

Cassie pranced away, leaving Jenna alone to reminisce about how much things had changed since her last birthday.

There was so much to be thankful for, not the least of which was her sister's love and support. She was surrounded by friends and family and about to begin a new chapter in her life with the man she loved.

As if conjured by her thoughts, Jenna heard the familiar sound of Bob's car pulling into the driveway and rushed to the door to greet him. He stepped out of the car holding a single pink carnation. The sight of him still made her knees weak. How did she ever get so lucky?

Bob met her at the doorway. He wrapped one arm around her waist and tugged her tight against his body. Their lips touched in a soft, sweet kiss. They lingered over it, knowing there'd be time to turn up the heat later.

"Just what I needed," Bob said, still holding her close. He raised one eyebrow and gave her a suggestive wink. Its wolfish appeal was lost behind the nerdy Clark Kent glasses. "Now if you'll reach into my pocket," he said, "you'll find your birthday gift."

"Oh, that again?"

He chuckled. "Stop, I'm trying to be adorable."

"You don't have to try very hard," she said, reaching into his pocket. She grasped a small box with a single ribbon tied around it. It couldn't be a ring. He'd given her an engagement ring for Christmas. So what . . . ?

"Go ahead, open it," he said. "I can't wait."

She untied the ribbon and opened the box. Inside was a key. An ordinary house key.

"Is this . . . ?"

"Yep, the key to our new home. It's going to need a lot of hard work and elbow grease, not to mention a small fortune in repairs, but soon it'll be . . ."—he lowered his voice dramatically—"the Mourningkill Bed-and-Breakfast, with your hosts Mr. and Mrs. Robert Hartwood."

Jenna squealed and jumped into his waiting arms. "This is the best gift ever. The start of our new life together." She buried her face alongside his neck, overflowing with happiness.

"And the best part is, we'll be able to move in right after the wedding," he said.

Wedding. The word still caught her by surprise, sending her emotions whirling with joy. "Perfect."

Bob set her down, and they walked inside, arms linked around each other's waists. Jenna reached in a cabinet for the bud vase that was always close by, filled it with water, and added the pink carnation. She set the vase on the table alongside the Dorothy figurine and placed the key beside it. The key to their new life. So far this was turning out to be her best birthday ever.

"Hey, what's all the noise in here?" Cassie came into the kitchen and gave Bob a peck on the cheek.

"We have the house," Jenna cried, pointing to the key on the table. "We can move in right after the wedding."

Cassie made a mock frown. "So, you're actually going through with it, huh?"

Bob put her in a gentle, brotherly head lock. "Yep, I'm taking her off your hands. You can have this house all to yourself now."

"Thank God," Cassie said, wrenching easily out of his grasp. "I thought she'd never leave."

Jenna looked at her and smiled. "I won't be far away," she said. "You know I'll never leave you all alonely."

Cassie reached out and took her sister's hand. "I know that."

A knock on the door distracted all three of them. "I'll get it, " Cassie said. "It's my door now. The two of you can have your own doorway to . . ."—she waved a hand in the air—"to wherever."

"Everwhen," Jenna murmured.

"I like that," Bob said. "Maybe we'll put that on a sign over the entrance. *Doorway to Everwhen*. It has a nice ring to it."

Jenna was only half listening. She watched as Cassie opened the door to a gray-haired woman who looked vaguely familiar.

"Hello, I'm your new neighbor," the woman said. "Maya is my name." She handed Cassie a foil-wrapped loaf. "Banana bread," she said. "I just made it this morning."

"Thank you," Cassie said. "Would you like to come inside? I'm Cassie, by the way."

"No, I just wanted to say hello and introduce myself. I'll stop by another time when it's more convenient."

Jenna stepped closer. "I'm Jenna," she said. "Do I know you?"

The woman's eyes twinkled. "Perhaps we've seen each other around town?"

"Maybe," Jenna said, not entirely convinced that was the case. Before she could question their new neighbor, however, Maya turned to leave. Jenna watched as she leaned close and whispered to Cassie, "If there's anything you need, just let me know."

Cassie returned the smile. "I will," she said.

Jenna frowned. Warning bells went off at the edge of her consciousness. There and then gone. She watched as Cassie closed the door behind the woman.

Something . . . something she should remember.

And just like that the thought disappeared. Jenna shrugged and walked to the oven to check on the duck. She filled the baster and coated the duck with drippings. It was coming along nicely.

While Cassie peeled potatoes, Jenna prepared a salad. It wasn't long before more guests came to the door. Diane walked in holding her toddler's hand. Dean followed behind carrying bags and bottles and baby equipment.

"Look who's walking like a big girl!" Jenna cried. "And don't you look adorable, Emily."

Emily wore a flowered headband to match her pink and white frilly dress, along with shiny black patent-leather shoes.

"Show Auntie Jenna what you have, honey," Diane coaxed.

Auntie Jenna. This was one of the most important things that had happened this past year: the gift of friendship. Diane had truly forgiven her, and now this precious child was a part of her life. She didn't deserve the title "Auntie," but hearing it filled her heart with love and pride.

Emily held out a gift. "Happy birdday," she said, holding out a black and white stuffed dog with a red ribbon for a collar.

"She picked it out herself," Diane explained.

"Oh, thank you, sweetie." Jenna bent down on one knee and held out her arms. "Come to auntie, Em." She scooped the baby into her arms and nuzzled her neck, making Emily giggle.

Diane smiled at Jenna as if to say, "Aren't we the lucky ones." Jenna couldn't agree more.

"When do we eat?" Dean asked. "I burn more calories lugging half our household around for the baby than I did playing football in college." He dropped dramatically into a kitchen chair. "I have to keep up my energy.

"Soon," Jenna said with a laugh. "We're just waiting for Parker."

"Parker, huh? Did he change his name?"

"No," Jenna replied. "He still goes by his adopted name professionally. But when he finally found his birth certificate and saw that Mom named him Parker . . . well, it just felt natural for us to call him by his given name."

Both Jenna and Cassie were still getting used to the idea of having a big brother. For so long it had just been the two of them. Once they'd found Parker, however, they'd embraced him with open arms. He and Cassie had fallen into good-natured bickering as if they'd grown up together. The truth was, they could barely remember a time when he wasn't there, teasing them and offering "older brother" advice whether they wanted it or not.

Bob glanced out the window. "Speaking of the devil," he said.

Cassie greeted Parker at the door. "Well, if it isn't the prodigal brother."

He rolled his eyes. "That's not even an accurate analogy."

He turned to Jenna and handed her a small jewelry box. "Happy birthday. Maybe this will make up for all the birthdays we've missed over the years."

Jenna opened the box and gasped with delight at the sculpted gold pendant. "Oh, Parker, it's lovely."

"The guy at the jewelry store called it the Tree of Life. It reminded me of you."

"Suck-up," Cassie murmured under her breath.

"Look," Parker said, ignoring Cassie. "I had him place our birthstones on the branches—me, you, and pain-in-the-ass over there."

"I love it," Jenna said, lifting the necklace over her head. "It's perfect." She was truly touched. As she brushed her fingers over the sculpted metal, a strong sense of déjà vu washed over her. She shivered, then turned away.

"I have a birthday coming up soon, too, you know," Cassie said. "I prefer silver and turquoise."

"Duly noted," Parker said with a wink.

Just then the kitchen timer sounded, and everyone rushed into action. Jenna took the duck out of the oven, while Bob found a knife to start carving. Cassie mashed the potatoes, Parker put the finishing touch on the salad, Dean set up the baby's booster seat, and Diane set the table.

Soon they were all gathered around, laughing and complimenting Jenna on the wonderful meal. It wasn't a Norman Rockwell painting, but it was perfect as far as Jenna was concerned. She couldn't imagine being any happier.

After dinner Cassie lit the candles on Jenna's birthday cake, and they all sang "Happy Birthday." Out of tune.

"Make a wish," Cassie said.

Jenna blew out the candles but didn't bother making a wish. Looking around the table at her friends and family, she knew with certainty that all of her wishes had already been granted. The words that came to mind couldn't be more true.

There really was no place like home.

THE END

Acknowledgments

To the Sisters of the Lake, Christine Wenger, Patricia Otto, Jo Piraneo, Sue Peterson, Barbara Parella, Joan Dermatis, Dorice Nelson, and Dar Scalera, who were there in the beginning.

To my TARA sisters for support and guidance along the way.

To my first readers, Geneva Brock and Denise Madigan, who boosted my confidence when it sagged.

To my fantastic agent, Linda Scalissi of 3 Seas Literary Agency, who believed in this book from the beginning, and Anna Paustenbach of HarperLegend, who gave it a home.

Thank you all. I couldn't have done it without you!

About the Author

LINDA BLESER is an author of traditional women's fiction with the twist of a what-if in each story. She started her career writing short stories for women's literary magazines and is the author of numerous women's fiction, romance, and thriller novels. Linda lives near Tampa, Florida. Visit her at lindableser.com.

Discover great authors, exclusive offers, and more at hc.com.

Made in the USA
Coppell, TX
04 June 2021

56813568R10142